BOOKS BY M K SCOTT

THE WEDDING CAKE BLUES

By
M K Scott

CHAPTER ONE

T HE SWEET, RICH smell of chocolate wafted from the oversized oven, dancing around stainless-steel appliances crammed into the tidy kitchen before slipping into the small waiting area where customers could wait patiently for their morning cup of Joe and a sweet treat. Della Delacroix arched a brow and strained her ears for any jingles of the mounted bell on the entry door indicating incoming or exiting customers. Not a sound—if she discounted her mother humming show tunes. If her mother was humming, it meant no customers. Della closed her eyes and sighed. Her hands settled on her hips as she circled her head, relieving the tension created by her constant downward glance while cooking. Her dark ponytail danced with the action.

Here she was within spitting distance of thirty, working hard to make her dream of owning a bakery a reality. It wasn't a bit like that movie where a guy built a ballpark and all the baseball greats of old came to play. She'd thought it would be enough to bake delicious cakes and pastries at reasonable prices to ensure a thriving business.

Her nose wrinkled, and her top lip curled at her former optimistic outlook about how easy running a bakery would be. The oven buzzer's shrill tone had her hurrying to check her chewy brownie cookies. Timing was everything—too long and they'd be dry. She donned mitts, opened the oven doors, received a blast of heat, and removed the finished cookies.

Her mother, Mabel, strolled into the room, placed her hands on her ample hips, and sniffed the air appreciatively. "Yummy. Gimme a sample."

"No, you don't," Della teased and pivoted, moving the tray of fragrant sweets out of her mother's reach. "Aren't you trying to lose weight for your dating profile pic?"

"Seriously! You act like you don't know me." Mabel jerked her chin upward ruffling her carefully dyed auburn curls. She gestured to her well-proportioned figure. "Haven't you heard men prefer women with a little padding?" A chuckle punctuated her comment before she sighed. "Besides, I think putting up a dating profile is a bit too soon for me." She pointed a manicured finger in Della's direction. "However, not you."

Not this again. It was the twenty-first century, and women could live full lives without marrying and having the usual two children. As a good daughter, Della chose not to mention she wasn't interested in dating. More accurately, she wasn't interested in anyone her mother, her friends, or distant relatives, thought were suitable for her. They never were.

"Mother, it's been seven years since Dad died. He'd want you to be happy."

A snort sounded, and Mabel narrowed her eyes. "If he wanted to make me happy, he would have taken better care of himself, ate better, and exercised."

Mabel waited until the cookie tray went onto the counter before picking up a spatula to lift off a freshly baked cookie. She missed the irony that she just complained about her deceased husband's eating habits while reaching for a calorie-rich goodie. A rapturous expression crossed her face as she chewed.

"This is good!" she declared. With her mouth still full, she reached for another cookie. "Really good."

The praise made Della smile. Compliments on her cooking were always appreciated. "Thanks, Mom. Maybe you could be my testimonial person for an ad. We have to get more people acquainted with our scrumptious fudgy brownie cookies."

"So true." Her mother agreed, giving an emphatic nod while gesturing with a cookie. "There's got to be something we can do. I didn't invest your father's insurance money just to watch it go down the drain."

The words made Della cringe. As the unexpected, only child who showed up as her mother approached forty and had given up all hope of procreating, her mother went out of her way to be the ultimate parent. Della had in no way intended for her cake decorating dreams to suck in her mother, too. Even though she never asked for help, Mabel insisted on forwarding her the money when the bank refused to do so. Businesses failed every day, but Della had no intention of being just another statistic.

She even came up with a cute name, Cupid's Catering Company. Maybe that was a mistake. People who wanted a simple cake, a donut, or even a fast lunch assumed a catering company didn't do basic food. A large wooden sign with the bakery name and tiny chubby cupids with rosy cheeks cavorting on it had cost her plenty. She couldn't afford to change the name on the sign or on her website. Her energy would be better served to concentrate on the catering side.

She took the spatula from her mother and used it to carefully maneuver the chocolate cookies onto lace doilies. "At least we have the McCormick/Lawson wedding coming up."

Mabel mumbled through a full mouth. "Bridezilla." Her accompanying eye-roll filled in the things she didn't say.

Dealing with Ellie McCormick for the last six weeks had not only added to Della's stress levels but had also caused tension headaches. Ellie had changed the menu at least five times. The upside was Della hadn't ordered too many of the supplies before each change. Other vendors had complained about the difficulty of working with Ellie. It meant it wasn't just Della. This time next month the wedding would be over, and she'd be getting bookings galore from wedding guests. A well-planned catering spread would serve as her audition for future brides and mothers of the brides-to-be.

"Remember! Two hundred of Owens' best people will be the guests."

Mabel snorted. "I've heard that a half-dozen times. You've probably heard it more."

"True." She placed the last cookie on the doily and lifted the tray to carry it into the front area. The breakfast crowd might be slow to non-existent, but their location close to the courthouse had many of the workers stopping in for a quick snack, with the cookies being a favorite.

"All I have to do is grin and bear it. I can handle difficult people as long as they have money in their grubby hands."

She tossed off the last words as she backed into the swinging door that separated the kitchen from the shop area. A slight clearing of a throat had her turning too fast causing the cookies to slide on her tray. Fortunately, she stopped the slide by placing the tray on the counter and smiled at the handsome, bearded man dressed in a pea coat suitable for the chilly, misty weather.

"How can I help you?"

He reached into his wallet, pulled out a ten-dollar bill and flourished it. "I got money in my grubby hand. Hope that means I can get a black coffee and something sweet. Those cookies you almost dropped might do the trick."

"Ah yes."

Color flooded her cheeks. Not only had the man overheard her remark, but he also hadn't hesitated to tease her. Some people might call it flirting. The thought had her crinkling her nose. Men didn't flirt with Della. That much she knew. All through school, her chunky physique earned requests to copy her homework as opposed to dates. Some of the less nice girls referred to her as thunder thighs and plus size nerd.

Once her baking skill emerged right around her junior year, her brownies were another thing in demand. Some mean girls joked she enjoyed her creations—too much. While she felt the need to sample, she didn't gorge herself. Nothing would make her into a waif-thin model. She'd seen the women on her mother's side of the family. Wide hips and generous proportions just happened to be the hand Fate had dealt her.

No reason to flirt back since nothing would come of it. She poured the coffee in a to-go cup without asking if he intended to stay. He struck her as someone who had places to be.

"Sweetheart, I've got a plan to help jumpstart your love life!" her mother called out before pushing the door open and seeing the sole customer. "Oh, sweet pea. I had no clue you were busy."

Somehow, she doubted that. Voices carried, but she hadn't heard the front door bell ring, either. "Not too busy." She smiled at her customer as she handed him the capped cup of coffee.

Her mother plopped her elbow on the counter and rested her chin in her upturned hand. "Hello. You look interesting. Where did you come from?"

Good heavens, not this again. The younger men Mabel chose to chat up probably thought her overfriendly overtures meant cougar city. In truth, her mother was shopping for Della as opposed to herself, which wasn't much better.

Della wrapped the cookie and stuck it into a white bakery bag. "Okay. That will be four dollars and twenty-seven cents."

Bearded and Handsome grinned as he handed over the ten-dollar bill. "Very reasonable. Hope the cookie is as delicious as it smells."

"It is." Some might call her cocky, but she knew her skills, and her fudgy brownie cookies were the best.

"I'll vouch for that," her mother offered and brushed at her mouth to rid herself of any crumbs that might reside. "I didn't catch your name. I thought I knew everyone worth knowing in town."

Would the ground just open and swallow Della? She forced a laugh. "My mom is such a jokester."

She shot her mother a significant look, hoping she'd tone down her attitude. As if expecting this, Mabel turned her head away from Della and focused on the stranger, who grinned at her. He arched an eyebrow, transferred the cookie bag and coffee to his left hand, and stretched out his right hand to Mabel. "I'm Ethan Stone. Pleased to meet you."

Mabel took the offered hand and gave it a hearty shake. "Pleased to meet you, Ethan. I'm Mabel Delacroix. You've already met my daughter, Della."

Ethan nodded convivially, cut his eyes to Della, and then back to Mabel.

Della could almost hear the wheels in his head turning, wondering why anyone would name their daughter Della Delacroix. "Expecting a boy, my parents somehow thought the name they had picked out, Jason, wouldn't serve for a girl."

"I would agree with that."

Her mother sniffed. "You always tell that story in such a judgy way. Please remember I was still under anesthesia. It took a while before I considered that your first name sounded a bit like your last. By then, it was too late."

She waved her hand to rid herself of any condemnation and tsked. "What you must think of us. Don't let me keep you from your big, important job."

He touched a finger to his temple. "I'm the one who should be blushing now. I came here to ask you questions pertinent to my case and ended up buying sweets and chatting. I'm a private investigator."

"What case? What questions?" Unease unfurled in Della's stomach like one of those resurrection plants you add water to, and they miraculously come to life. Her water tended to be the unknown and uncertain, which often were the same.

"Jeffrey Lawson. Have you seen him lately?" The words hung in the air, changing the former light-hearted atmosphere.

As the potential groom of Bridezilla, Della had seen him squirm as Ellie complained about how provincial their sample menus were. A dazed look had settled on him when Ellie changed the menu for the fourth time. Most of the time, the well-groomed heir to Lawson Industries acted as if he'd rather be anywhere else other than listening to his fiancée rage against the world and threaten financial as well as legal repercussions if she wasn't satisfied.

"Well, I have seen him. Maybe a week ago. He was with Ellie."

Ethan shook his head and grimaced. "Not good. You were the last wedding vendor I've contacted. I hoped you might know something the others didn't. Thanks, anyhow."

His brow furrowed as he worked out whatever issue was troubling him. Both Mabel and Della held up a hand in farewell, but he never even noticed. Ethan exited, clutching his bakery bag and coffee.

Della waited until the door closed before speaking. "Now I'm worried there might not be a wedding. The man probably hightailed it after the fourth menu change."

"Could be," her mother agreed. "It's more likely his family had him kidnapped to prevent the nuptials."

Out of the two of them, Della considered her thought to be the more practical one. Only this time, her mother might be right.

Even though it might be selfish on her part, she needed this wedding. After insisting the menu couldn't be changed again, Ellie McCormick had agreed to the final menu. However, Bridezilla could still try.

"There's only one thing we can do—find Jeffrey Lawson."

Her mother rested one hand on her hip and regarded her daughter with disbelief. "How are we supposed to do that? It seems to me Ethan is doing that now, and he doesn't sound like he's having much luck. Why would *we* succeed when he hasn't?"

Normally, she'd be the naysayer, but she *needed* to cater this event and earn the money it provided. Della walked over to her mother and hooked arms with hers. "We make a great team in the bakery and out. We are not without skills. Didn't we both live with one of the county's best detectives?"

"Your father was second to none." A smile danced across her mother's face as her eyes rolled upward, remembering. "Still," she gave a slight sniff, "Owens is far from big city crime. Many of the crimes he solved were partially due to information gathered from my gossip hotline."

Her mother tapped her head, reminiscent of how her father had done and lowered her voice to imitate the man. "Fred Lowenstein is missing his brand-new Mercury sedan. Who does your gossip hotline like for it?"

"Dad couldn't arrest someone based on gossip!" The revelation that her father had asked her mother for local gossip stunned, but she knew from her obsession with crime dramas and mysteries that the casual observer knew a great deal.

"No, he didn't arrest them on gossip." Mabel's crow's feet gathered at the corners of her eyes as she chuckled, making her resemble a cheerful gnome minus the beard. "He checked them out, did the legwork, and sometimes the gossip proved right. If nothing else, it was a good starting point. The person of interest usually threw someone else under the bus." Her shoulders went up in a shrug. "In the end, your father got his man, or in some cases, woman. I think he may have thought you'd follow in his footsteps."

Memories of donning one of her father's cast-off suit jackets and brandishing an oversized magnifying glass when she was ten took shape in her mind. Her father used to call her his junior detective and even give her missions to find things. Usually, it was objects such as missing car keys, tickets to an upcoming baseball game, or the remote he had misplaced and, on a few occasions, he even laid out clues for her to decipher. It boosted her confidence in her investigative skills so much that she volunteered to discover who had helped themselves to the money from the scout bake sale.

The troop's original intention had been to give the money to the local animal shelter. Della deduced the possible thief was also her fellow scout at the time, the only one left alone with the money who suddenly had a large supply of junk food she hadn't brought with her. Rather than turn her in, Della managed to convince the girl to return the money minus the six dollars or so she'd already spent at the nearby convenience store. The incident ended her love of investigation and scouting.

The other scouts and leaders assumed she was the culprit. Despite knowing her and how hard she worked for the troop, they immediately fingered her for the crime, which made her want nothing to do with them in the future. Of course, her parents wanted to intervene, but Della wanted none of it. The light-fingered scout stayed in the troop and possibly gossiped about the incident, naming Della as the thief.

While she might not have said the actual words, Della swore off all investigative pursuits after experiencing the way they could come back and bite you. Now, though, if she didn't do something, her hopes and dreams would blow up like her scouting efforts.

"Dad was the best," Della admitted, returning to the conversation. She crossed her arms and leaned against the counter. "That doesn't mean everyone else is stellar."

"Have to admit, I've never found anyone as special as him."

Della arched her eyebrows over the comment. As far as she knew, her parent hadn't even considered dating, let alone remarriage. "I assume you're talking about detective work as opposed to husband."

"Both," her mother corrected and turned away.

Now, she'd gone and made her mother cry. Whenever she turned away like that, it was to hide a tear. Time to change the subject or at least steer it away from her father. She pushed off the counter. "I've read most people assume everyone else thinks like they do or works as hard as they do. That's why they're puzzled by those who don't."

Her mother turned, her mascara smudged at the corner of her right eye. Forcing a smile, she asked, "This is leading where?"

"We assume everyone we meet works as hard as we do. What if they don't? Come on, think about it. You've got plenty of people bragging about how they graduated at the top of their class, which may or may not be true. Some of us must have lawyers, doctors, accountants, etc., who graduated at the bottom of their class."

Mabel held out her hand, palm out in a halt gesture. "I'd rather not think about that." Her nose crinkled. "Makes me uneasy. Are you saying half our town isn't any good at their professions?"

"Maybe not half. Some of those bottom of the classers moved elsewhere. You have to admit some are better than others." She waited for her mother to acknowledge that with a head bob. "This goes for any profession. Maybe Ethan looks the part, but he doesn't have the investment we do in locating Lawson. Let him do his thing. We do ours. As far as tracking a missing man, you've got a gossip hotline second to none that can throw light on why the man is nowhere to be found."

Her mother sniffed. "I may be good, but it doesn't take a genius to understand why Lawson is making himself scarce. He's found himself hogtied to Ellie McCormick. I'd chew my leg off to get away."

Della held up her hand. "You have a point, but it has to be more than that. Why hire an investigator? We need to find out why the man ran off? Or even whom the man ran off *to*? Or where?"

Her mother's expression morphed from doubtful to curious. "That does sound up my alley. What's your role?"

"Analytical, of course. We know why he ran—mostly. I need to figure out how to allay his fears, get him back, and save our event." Even though her words were bold, Della had no clue how it would work, but work it had to since this was her first wedding catering job.

"Count me in!" her mother chimed.

CHAPTER TWO

A FIRM TUG on the fitted jacket of Della's go-to business suit didn't release the pinch it had on her waist. It was hard to believe she used to don business attire and head out to work at the mortgage company where she'd delighted, dismayed, or sometimes confused people when she called to report the progress of their application. As for the suit, she'd only worn that to the job interview and a funeral some five years ago. Not that they both happened at the same time, but close enough that the suit served both occasions. Maybe she should have gone with the shapewear her mother recommended or better yet, worn something different.

The sound of a car door closing echoed throughout the cavernous parking garage. *Spooky.* Plenty of thriller movies had people attacked in empty car garages late at night. Even though the sunlight didn't penetrate to sub-basement B or E or whatever it was, it remained daylight above ground. Besides, Lawson Industries, ranking as one of the prime American innovators in business and educational software, had plenty of cars that packed the level.

She might as well get going and find out whatever she could before disappearing for an extra-long lunch to work the bakery crowd. She stepped out with purpose, but her unaccustomed heels made her lurch rather like a reanimated corpse in a low-grade horror movie. Geesh, it was hard to believe people dressed like this every day to go to work. Swift footsteps had her stepping out of the way when a man clad in blue jeans, a hoodie, and carrying cardboard holder loaded with coffee cups buzzed past her.

The combined aromas of a dark Columbian blend, a pumpkin spice latte, along with the deeper heavier note of chocolate wafted behind him. It could be a hot chocolate or someone who enjoyed an extra sweetness to their brew. A single clear note of honey had her wondering if there was a tea included. She stood, inhaling the scent long after the man vanished. Being able to separate ingredients served as her superpower. It still didn't measure up to being able to jump buildings in a single bound, but it *did* serve with folks who refused to part with a particular recipe.

The hurrying man's clothes made her question if he worked there or was simply a java delivery dude. Must be the latter. After all, software folks had to make more than a humble baker, which equaled a more elevated attire than the athletic shoes and white cotton chef coats she bought online. Mentally, she ran through how she'd greet the first official employee she saw.

Good morning. I'm Della. I'm the Customer Support Advantage temp from the agency.

Truthfully, she didn't expect to get a job at Lawson Industries. She'd applied at the temp service a few weeks before when a lack of steady customers threatened her bottom line. Her mother agreed to serve as day staff if she did land a temp job. In the end, she told herself it would be for a very short time. As soon as the McCormick/Lawson wedding happened, she'd have plenty of deposits from pre-bookings that would allow her to forgo any side hustle. Then out of the blue, the agency called, shortly after she announced her intentions to hunt Lawson down. Was it serendipity? Hard to say, but it might serve all the same.

The agency told her it had something to do with answering the phone, which was better than the software engineer and front-end specialist. No way could she fake her way through the last two positions. Her experience with customer service consisted of listening to staticky music while on hold and often being disconnected. That she *could* do. Her lips twisted as she considered the last word in the title—*Advantage*. It sounded like a bit more than putting someone on hold until they hung up on their own. If she could comp people stuff, that would be sweet. Usually, though, that privilege belonged to the manager.

A thirty-ish woman in khakis and a polo rushed by with her hand resting on the messenger bag draped across her body. Probably a courier who carried needed forms to different agencies. Was everyone in a hurry today? Della checked her phone for the time and received a shock. Her moment analyzing coffee, then speculating about her temp job ate into the cushy time buffer she'd given herself. Better get a move on it before she lost her fake job.

Even though her only purpose in taking the temp job was to find out more about the missing Lawson heir, the money she'd earn in the process would be a much-needed help. So far, she'd made rent on time but only because her landlord allowed her to pay online. A few times, her payment had posted minutes before midnight on the final day. Creating cakes and memorable sweets appeared to be a feast or famine prospect. Mainly, all she'd endured so far was the famine side.

When her fresh cookies and pastries didn't sell immediately, she'd mark them down as day-old pastries. After that, they became part of her diet, which might explain the suit's tightness. Della blew out a long breath as she struck out with a bold step, only to wobble horribly. Whoever thought of high heels had to be a sadist.

The stainless-steel parking lot elevator gleamed like a beacon in the distance. All she had to do was reach it. "I can do this." She hissed the words as if to encourage her ankle and heels to be on better terms.

"Yes, you can," a feminine voice commented, causing Della to pivot, almost twisting her ankle in the process. For a second she wavered, pitching forward, close to kissing the ground, which was the last thing she needed. *Don't fall. I don't have time for this.*

Despite telling herself not to fall, the ground rushed up at her until a hard yank on her left arm stopped her descent.

"Goodness!" An unfamiliar, heavy-set woman pulled Della back into a standing position and shook her head. "You need to get rid of those shoes or learn to walk in them."

"Ah, thank you." Color climbed into her face as she faced her rescuer. "I appreciate your help. Good advice about the shoes, but I doubt if I'll ever be able to walk in them."

"I hear you." A wide smile brightened the woman's already pleasant expression as she held out her hand in greeting. "I'm Tyesha. You new here?"

"It depends on how fast I get upstairs and report for my temp job. Could be I'll be fired before I even show up for work." Sadly, her words could be prophetic.

"Oh really?" Interest flickered in Tyesha's eyes. "There's a half-dozen temp positions open at Lawson. You wouldn't happen to be the new software engineer?"

"Not hardly." She grimaced. "Not part of my skill set. I'd love to talk, but I need to get going. Don't want to make a bad impression on my future boss."

"Understandable." Tyesha fell in step with Della but had to slow her own gait to do so. "What position are you here for?"

"Customer Support Advantage. I was told it was mainly answering the phones."

The two of them had managed to get about three yards closer to the elevator. There were six or so yards left between her and the gleaming box that would give her feet a break. It was hard to believe some women donned even higher heels. They had to be an entirely different species than Della. It could be their feet were shaped for heels like the Barbie dolls she had as a kid.

Another person sprinted past them toward the elevator. Tyesha called to him, "You'd better hold that elevator!"

Once the three of them were enclosed in the mirrored interior, smelling slightly of smoke, Tyesha nodded at the kid in the hoodie who had held the elevator for them. "Don't look so worried, Todd. I'll tell Ryan you were with me talking about the project rollout."

Todd blinked twice, and then shook his head. "Why would you be talking to me about the rollout?"

Wait a minute. Della gave the male a thorough once over from his unshaven face, which included pillow creases in his cheek, to his bed head, which meant he hadn't been awake too long. He didn't look older than seventeen, but Tyesha talked like he worked there. Come to think of it, the woman acted as if she was in a position of authority. The sleepy employee missed the offered excuse for his tardiness.

Tyesha snorted. "Jump on it, Todd. Not too many people would be that kind."

The elevator bell rang before the doors opened. Todd shot Della a confused glance. "Who are *you*?"

Before Della could refer to herself as a temp, Tyesha answered for her. "She's a newbie like you, but I have a feeling she might end up being one of Lawson's best employees."

Wow. It was kind of Tyesha to say so, but she had to wonder if it were a bit of a joke. So far, she had done nothing to impress anyone. Her inability to walk in heels was the only thing she had demonstrated so far. Maybe Tyesha was one of those people who said positive things to get people to try to live up to the good hype. That had to be it.

Todd jumped out of the elevator and vanished down one of the corridors that veered off to the right. Hard to say if he'd take advantage of the gracious offer. She smiled at Tyesha as she stepped onto the carpeted hallway. "Guess this is where we part company. I do appreciate your help."

Sounds of typing along with chatter drifted from different directions. While there were some number plates with arrows adhered to the wall, it did nothing to inform Della what direction Customer Support Advantage might be located. "Um, would you happen to know where the temps report?"

"You come with me. I'll even introduce you to your new boss." Tyesha gestured to the nearest right hall and turned toward it. She cast a glance over her shoulder to assure herself Della followed.

"I'm coming," Della offered. "You know, *the shoes.*"

"You'll have to lose those. You can kick them off under your desk. Don't let me see you wearing those again."

"Okay," Della agreed, not sure why her newfound friend threw out commands like a general. If there was a tomorrow at Lawson's, she'd not be wearing the torture devices squeezing her toes and biting her heels. A nice pair of black ballet flats would serve as footwear.

They turned again and entered an open space sectioned off by half wall cubicles. Della's standing position allowed her to see into the workspaces where employees typed on their laptops. A few had their phone wedged between their shoulder and cheek, while others sported a blank look that meant either caffeine or inspiration or possibly both were in short supply.

Most called out to Tyesha, usually with *good morning* or a similar salutation. One man nodded in Della's direction and asked, "You're not going to scare this one off, too?"

"Hush." Tyesha waved the remark away and nudged Della. "Ignore him. He has a reputation for saying mean things."

Since Tyesha delivered this tidbit in her normal voice, everyone heard her, including the man. "Doesn't mean they aren't true," he called back.

Tyesha's pace picked up, forcing Della to struggle to keep up. "Um, my boss. I assume you know him or her."

"I do."

"Could you tell me anything useful? I want to do a good job." At least good enough to hang around to get the needed information on the Lawson heir.

"Admirable," Tyesha commented as she made a sharp turn into another cubicle lined area. Phones chirped, but only two people populated the half-dozen spaces and both were on the phone. They managed head bobs as Tyesha steamed by, pulling Della in her wake.

"As for your boss, if you do a decent job and aren't sneaking out for a smoke break every ten minutes, you should be fine."

"I don't smoke."

"You're sounding like the model employee already." Tyesha pulled out a chair from a cleared desk. "Here's your desk."

Curving lines gave the white metal desk a modern feel. Della sat, happy to give her feet a break. "All right. I still haven't met my boss, and I don't know what to do."

"You *have* met your boss." Tyesha's lips lifted into a wide grin as she used her thumb to indicate herself. "Got some papers you need to fill out for personnel. Lori will train you after."

"That sounds good." Although Della couldn't say *how* good it sounded since she was too busy reviewing the last ten minutes. Had she done anything horrible or said anything inappropriate?

A sheaf of papers landed on her desk, which took some time. By the time she had filled out each paper with her full name and address, the nearest employee scooted her chair over.

A tall, thin woman with dark roots noticeable on her blonde hair spoke. "Hello, I'm Lori." Her nose wrinkled as if she'd heard something funny. "I'm supposed to train you. Not sure if it deserves the glorified title." The woman tucked a lock of hair behind one ear and the corners of her mouth lifted slightly, possibly trying for a smile, but hadn't informed her face.

"I'm Della. I'll do my best to catch on as quickly as possible."

She pushed as much cheer as she could into the statement. Her mother's constant refrain mentioned catching more bees with honey than vinegar. What she needed was people to like her enough to share any gossip.

No one would ever hire her to guess people's age at the carnival, but she assumed Lori might be a year or two older than herself. If nothing else, they had age in common, which meant they lived through similar incidents. Hopefully, Della could springboard that into a talking point.

Lori groaned and commented over one shoulder to the only other employee in the room. She didn't even try to lower her voice to prevent Della from hearing. "We got another Pollyanna. I doubt she'll last through lunch."

Although, her intentions were to get the information and run back to the bakery, a challenge had been issued, even if it had been done inadvertently. She tamped down her sunny attitude and said, "I'll be here after lunch. Just show me the basics."

"I'm liking you better already." Lori pointed to the desk phone loaded with buttons. "People call to complain about Lawson software they bought that doesn't work. Usually, they want to yell or cuss at you. We may answer the phone with a smile in our voice, which you could do very well, but we are not techs. We can't answer any software related questions. The best we can do is de-escalate them a tad before dumping them on a tech who will probably tell them to turn the computer off and back on."

"Does turning off the computer and turning it back on ever work?" She had heard the line so often that it had become fodder for jokes.

Lori shrugged. "Not my rodeo. Let me show you how to transfer to Tech. Keep in mind that they seldom answer, which causes the person to hang up and call again, only madder than they were before."

Della had a feeling she knew why the other temps had left. Still, she reminded herself the others didn't have a bakery and catering business to support that rested on finding the elusive heir.

CHAPTER THREE

D ELLA PUSHED THE receive button on her headset only to hear a man on the other end grumble, "I've been on this phone for a good ten minutes."

She pressed her lips together to keep from saying something about it being impossible since she picked up the phone on the second ring. Even though her original intention consisted of putting in a few hours, getting the information on the missing bridegroom, and then disappearing, possibly with a lame excuse about picking up a relative from the airport, she couldn't do it. The number one reason being her mother didn't raise her that way. Then there was the central problem that so far, she hadn't heard anything except the phones ringing non-stop and snarky remarks from the overworked employees.

A ticklish sensation danced across her shoulder blades, a feeling she equated with being watched. Della forced her lips into a smile while remembering a comment that the caller could tell if she was smiling or frowning. "I'm so sorry for your wait. What can I do for you?"

After listening to a long, rambling complaint, she happily informed the man, "That's a technical matter. I'm switching you over to the Tech Department."

Cursing erupted from her headset as she punched in the number for Tech. On her first half dozen calls, she felt bad about sending the call to another department, especially if Tech just ignored it. After a couple of hours of unhappy, whiney callers, her reluctance to pass the call on disappeared.

Lori, who showed her the basics of working in the Customer Support Advantage, had also given the types of callers names, such as Lonely Single, Grumpy Grandparent, Clueless, and Tenacious Troll. The Lonely Single name covered anyone who called just to hear another human voice. Back when operators were actual people as opposed to automation, a simple inquiry for a phone number could serve that purpose. Grumpy Grandparent didn't have to be someone who was a senior citizen, but anyone who didn't understand the technology. As for Clueless, it could often be a wrong number. So far, she answered calls from two people who wanted to order pizzas. As for the Troll, she hoped she didn't get any of those calls that started with inquiries about her wardrobe.

Lori uncapped her marker and turned her chair in Della's direction. "What did you get?"

"Grumpy Grandparent, I suppose." His general attitude confirmed it.

The permanent marker squeaked as Lori made a tally mark on her whiteboard. The group kept track of the number of calls that came in a day. Too bad every caller was put into a group with a less than pleasant connotation.

"Do we have an expression for an ordinary person who calls with an issue?"

The question made sense to Della, but the look Lori settled for made her wonder if she had suggested having live grasshoppers for lunch.

"We don't. An ordinary person knows how to use the software and wouldn't call." Lori spun her chair around while simultaneously answering the phone. "Customer Support Advantage. Lori speaking. How may I serve you?"

How effortless Lori made it look. Della had a suspicion the woman couldn't stand most of the callers or her job for that matter. The possibility made Della sigh. Working in a similar atmosphere for a living had set her dreaming about owning a business as opposed to working for a corporation. Here she was doing the thing she didn't like, but only so she could keep the bakery running.

The call center needed more help since there was no downtime for gossip. Any break they received was one at a time. A mighty slim one allowed Della enough time to dash down to the hallway to the restroom to text her mother. Unfortunately, as a non-millennial, her mother not only didn't carry her cell on her person but could also go for hours without looking at it. The bakery could be flooded with customers or burning down for all she knew. More likely, her mother would be fielding single orders for coffee or hot chocolate as the courthouse workers showed up for their shifts.

Todd, the young man she'd met in the elevator, poked his head around the cubicle. "Heading out to the sandwich shop. Anyone need anything?"

Jaime, the other customer service representative, shook her head and managed to mime carrying a sack lunch so as not to interrupt her call.

Lori grimaced. "I brought my lunch. Nothing to get excited about. How about picking me up a six-inch meatball hero?"

A course in business psychology taught Della that people tended to prefer people who were like them. She waved her hand. "Make that two meatball subs."

The problem was she wasn't a fan of meatballs, especially when they were crammed into a hoagie bun. She wanted to call back her order as soon as she said it, but how would she get Lori to think they were simpatico unless they ate the same sandwich? A gossipy tidbit might slip as marinara sauce dripped down her chin and onto her only suit. It could just be enough information to put her on the trail of the Lawson heir.

Of course, she'd have to pay Todd. Lori handed him a twenty, making Della wonder how much the subs cost. Not that much, she hoped. A quick search of her purse yielded her wallet that contained a paltry five-dollar bill and four wrinkled ones. She held up the money with an uncertain smile.

The male staffer took the money and raised his eyebrows. "Cutting it a little close, aren't you?"

Since she had no clue what the hoagie cost, it was hard to know how to answer. "I'll pay you back tomorrow. What would I owe you?"

"Nothing," he grinned. "Just teasing you."

"Enough chatter. Go get lunch," Lori announced in an authoritative tone, then gentled her voice as she took a call.

"You got it." Todd left the area with a simple turn, even though his conversation with other employees floated back. Less than thirty minutes later, the food arrived, and the customer service team broke for lunch. Surprisingly, everyone ate at once in a conference room, including Todd. Her supervisor, Tyesha, explained the meal could serve as an organization meeting, too. That, unfortunately, would be no help with the missing groom.

Della did her best to make inroads with the sandwich she did not want. The problem was the more she chewed, the more the bread expanded in her mouth. She had half a mind to spit it into the trash while no one was watching. The marks of poor-quality bread were its uneven color, poor taste, and gaping airholes. A hearty sandwich deserved an equally robust bread. Something like a French baguette or even some thick Italian garlic bread. Sourdough would work, too. Her pickiness about her bread selection may have been what propelled her into making her own bread. Instead of fantasizing about what she'd rather be eating, she needed to swallow to be part of the conversation.

So far, she'd contributed nothing and only listened to Tyesha run down some figures from last week and the goals for this week. Jaime casually inserted she'd been on a date the night before. All eyes turned toward the quiet woman with open curiosity. Lori was the first to respond.

"Loser or keeper?"

Deciding if a man was worth seeing after one date alone sounded a bit harsh, even though Della knew she had done the same, especially when someone had ambushed her with a blind date. It would be interesting to see how Jaime responded.

A shy smile brightened her expression. "I'm not sure I'd call him a keeper, but he definitely isn't a loser. He reminds me a little of Mr. Lawson as far as manners, and he's about the same height and coloring."

"Well then," Tyesha held up one finger and waved it, "You'd better keep an eye on him and make sure he doesn't disappear."

Interesting. The staff knew about Jeffrey Lawson being among the missing. The appearance of a private eye had made her think it was a hush-hush matter. "Excuse me."

Before she could say anything else, Todd jumped in. "Come on! Who wouldn't run for the hills with that harpy he's got riding him?

When she first showed up at the office, I thought wow until she opened her mouth."

When Della had first met Ellie McCormick, she hadn't been surprised the woman had snagged the most eligible bachelor in town. The thought had depressed her, especially since Jeffrey Lawson struck her as a perfectly decent sort of guy. She'd assumed an intelligent male could see past the painted veneer into the ugly interior. Even though the beauty queen reeked of high maintenance, she was still the image of glossy perfection from the crown of her artistically highlighted hair to her French manicured toenails.

With one word, Ellie made Della question her profession. That word was *help*. Not in the usual could-you-help-me request, but rather a rant about her feelings about wedding help in the surrounding county. It didn't take long for Della to figure out she was talking about the various business owners who contracted out for weddings. Apparently, they were the help, and Ellie saw herself as an aristocrat. It made her wonder if she treated everyone the same. "What did she say?"

A snort erupted from Todd. "Basically, since she was marrying the boss, she'd be our boss, too."

"Stop now!" Tyesha made a low groan to accompany her sentiment.

"From what I heard," Jaime inserted with a spoonful of yogurt only inches from her mouth, "she's a beauty school dropout and knows nothing about software."

That explained the hair and possibly the toenails. It looked like Todd got the ball rolling and all Della had to do was listen.

"True," Todd agreed and opened his bag of chips. "It didn't stop her from giving out orders, though. She sent me out for a pumpkin spice latte. When she got it, she took one sip and threw it away. Said it wasn't made right. If that wasn't enough, she didn't even pay me for it."

"You should have asked Mr. Lawson for the money," Lori informed him with a nod.

"I could have." He shrugged his shoulders. "Felt stupid for fetching and carrying. I won't make that mistake again."

Was he referring to not getting coffee for Bridezilla or acting like an overeager puppy in the presence of a conventional beauty? Any other person would have said something by now. "Is Mr. Lawson missing?"

Tyesha held a finger up to her lips. "We may have been talking out of turn. I imagine it isn't unusual for a man to need some time for himself when making a life-changing decision."

The pained expression that accompanied the remark could be taken several ways. If the whole thing was a rom-com movie, then Tyesha would be secretly in love with her boss, and somehow, they'd get together before he tied the knot.

"Life changing? Hah!" Todd crunched a chip and smirked. "His wild days will be over." He paused, and then shook his head. "Most men would be having a last-minute fling. It could be he hooked up with an old flame and headed to the Caribbean."

Tyesha cleared her throat. "That's enough speculating about our boss. Della's going to get the wrong impression. Besides, if something were going on, his assistant, Barbie, would know."

Barbie? Really? She imagined a woman similar to the doll with a minuscule waist and a painted-on smile. It might explain how he ended up with Ellie. Well, her fellow employees weren't much help. What she needed was to reach Barbie, who might inadvertently reveal something. With no boss in the office, the woman could be bored.

"Where is Mr. Lawson's office?"

Lori shot her a narrow-eyed look. "Are you going to tattle on us?"

That was an odd question considering most employees talked about their boss. It indicated the meatball sandwich on subpar bread hadn't made them fast friends. "No. Why would I? There's nothing to tell. Besides, I don't know anyone higher up. Just curious, that's all. I always heard the CEOs of companies had palatial offices more like high-rise apartments."

Even though Della thought her explanation was a good save, Lori gave a dismissive sniff, allowing Tyesha to answer her inquiry.

"It's on the top floor. Nothing special, though. Dear old dad had the whole floor as his office. I heard it was something to see. He had a desk the size of a tank. Full bar and oversized furniture. Even had live trees in the place and a grand piano. Not sure about the piano, though. No one was allowed on the twentieth floor. The elevator had a special key to reach the penthouse."

She shook her head before continuing. "The younger Lawson cut up the humongous space into several units, including a research and development lab, Barbie's private office, another conference room, and of course, his own office. Kind of a shame, though. I mean, what's the use of being the boss if you don't have some spectacular office?"

Even though it would be tricky, Della knew she needed to talk to Barbie or better yet, get into Lawson's office. On all the old British mysteries, people were conveniently leaving messages on their calendars where they might be going or were last seen.

Life as a baker, no matter how many cop shows she watched or how many games she played with her detective father, didn't exactly prepare her for skullduggery, but she'd find a way.

CHAPTER FOUR

T HE MINUTE HAND on the analog clock in the customer service area moved with a jerky motion and a loud click. Surely a place that manufactured software would at least have a digital clock, but apparently not. Another shudder brought the hand to half-past four. Tyesha popped out of her office, waved at the group, and announced she had to leave for her child's school function.

Lori waited about a minute before ending a call and powered down her computer. She stood, stretching with her fingers interlaced over her head. "See ya tomorrow."

Della waved at her as she contemplated the possibility of people having staggered shift times. Perhaps each person left at a different time. The temp agency indicated she worked until five. What if she was the last one left answering phones? She wiggled in her seat and cut her eyes to Jaime, who calmly explained to her caller that she didn't have the ability to refund money for time wasted trying to learn how to use the software. With a polite goodbye, she disconnected and swung around in Della's direction.

"You know, everyone leaves early with the boss not being here. I'm not even sure how many people are still in the building."

"Ah…" She wanted to ask how a business could survive with employees leaving whenever they pleased. That wouldn't make her popular, so she said nothing.

As if Jaime could hear her thoughts, the twenty-something woman crinkled her pert nose. "No one leaves *too* early. Some come in earlier than their regular times instead. Most want to get a jump on traffic. I won't be staying much longer. You'll need to walk out with me because I have to lock up the office."

Good point. Couldn't have a newbie running around the office getting into who knows what. *Wait a minute.* If everyone was leaving it would be the perfect time to check out the missing bridegroom's office or possibly catch Barbie off guard. It might not take much if the woman matched up to the doll with the same moniker. Perhaps she was a long-legged beauty with perfect hair and permanent makeup hired as window dressing as opposed to having actual skills. Her lips twisted as she considered the company known for the famous icon was currently trying to make average looking dolls, which equated broader hips, cheekbones, and flat feet. Besides, she knew well enough judging someone by their name didn't always work. When people heard the name Della, they immediately thought of a sassy senior citizen. All the same, she couldn't return home with nothing to show for her efforts.

"Sounds like a plan to me. Should I come back tomorrow?" With Tyesha tearing out of the place the way she did, it was unclear if extra days were coming Della's way.

Laughter greeted her inquiry. "Please come back. If you have some friends willing to work, bring them, too. We are so under-staffed. Lawson Industries is an international company and currently we have three people in our department. Four, if you come back tomorrow."

"Can do." It didn't mean she'd get any more information. On the catering front, she should be making the tiny quiches and meatballs ahead of time. She could just pop them in the freezer and defrost the day before. Still, if there was no wedding, she had no reason to bother.

"Hey, just curious..." She prefaced her question, trying not to sound suspicious. It was right up there with asking for a friend. "Your research and development people. Do they wear lab coats like in the movies?"

Jaime's hand reached up to rub her neck as her brow furrowed. "I don't know. Most of us tend to stay in our own departments. I guess they could be running around in white lab coats. Why?"

Della shrugged. "No reason." It was time to distract from her obvious interest. "How do you shut off the computer?"

Talk about lame. It made her sound like she was a hundred years old and had never seen a PC. Jaime willingly talked her through the simple operation. As the screen flickered to black, Jaime gave her a nod. "Stay long enough and you'll get your own password."

It had possibilities, but it wouldn't be enough to allow her to delve into the details she wanted. With a grimace, Della reached for the shoes she had kicked off. "I wish I didn't have to wear these."

"Then don't. No one looks at your feet because they're all too busy leaving. I bet we won't see more than three people on our way out. Word of advice for tomorrow—wear something comfortable. No one sees us, which means we can wear what we want." Jaime gestured to her khaki pants and flower-strewn T-shirt. A pair of colorful athletic shoes completed her outfit.

"I will." She swung her purse over one shoulder and carried her shoes in the other hand.

Jaime turned off the lights and locked the door with a simple thumb twist lock. She must have noticed Della's attention because she explained the easily opened lock.

"Not much to steal inside there. Surely you noticed everything is fairly dated. Anyhow, there's a security system and guards."

"Guards?" Della echoed the word, aware that her plan to sneak upstairs as a research and development person didn't include guards. "I didn't see any this morning."

"Of course not. They don't come on until five. No reason for them to be here when the building is full of people." They both padded down a dimly lit hallway. The cubicles on either side were already abandoned and dark. When the boss was away, quitting time became fluid for most.

Away from the phone headset, Jaime chattered about her cat named Sebastian and the various sushi places in the area while rating them. Della managed the appropriate responses while she considered her clean white chef smock in the car. Early on, she decided an extra chef smock in the car would serve her well since cooking could be messy. A chocolate smeared top wasn't the image she wanted. That *could* work for a lab coat if someone saw her from a distance. It might not even be an issue if no one was around.

At the garage level, Jaime bid her goodbye and strolled to an older compact car. Della walked to her car, having no reason to hide. On the passenger side hung her clean smock. She scrunched down and peered through the window glass to be sure her co-worker had driven off. The suit jacket went into the car along with the shoes. No way was she going to wear those shoes now. However, a barefoot research person might cause talk. A hurried search through her car yielded a pair of flip flops, which would not pass any kitchen safety or hygiene inspection, but she could walk in them.

She buttoned up her smock over her shell, wiggled out of her hose, and slipped on the flip flops. All she could hope for was no one would see her. Della glanced around the empty garage before making an awkward dash for the lobby. If Lawson Industries were like most businesses, the doors would automatically lock after business hours. Her hand grasped the door handle, and she caught her breath before trying it. Amazingly, it swung open.

So far, so good. Della hit the elevator button. The silver doors slid open, revealing a yawning employee who shot her a curious glance as he exited. Not knowing how to respond, she stepped into the elevator and pressed the close button. Her eyes scanned over the buttons until she reached twenty, which she pushed. The elevator gave a little jump and then stopped, causing Della's heart to stop. The last thing she needed was to get stuck in the elevator, especially with no reason to be there.

With a mechanical grumble, the elevator continued its upward ascent. After what felt like forever, the doors opened to an expanse of glass, revealing a sun dropping in the west. Overseeing a big company had its perks. Clear panels served as walls to create rooms, while not obstructing the view. Clever. It made her wonder who thought of it. Lawson or possibly a construction supervisor had preserved the view while delineating the space.

Her admiration ended once she figured out that if she could see into the rooms, anyone inside could also see her. A brace of large palms served as her screen as she ducked behind them. From behind the feathery fronds, she surveyed the area. In the biggest area were some high tables. A few had laptops. A whiteboard had been set up on an easel alongside an extra-wide monitor. Modernistic chairs made of curving lines and minimally cushioned sat in a semicircle as if a discussion had just taken place. It had to be the research office.

Della straightened up to relieve the ache in her back at the same time as a door groaned open. Oh no! A reflexive knee bend had her peering out through the leaves. The white chef smock should stand out like a flag, except the sun behind her would flood the area with light, possibly allowing her to blend in. For the most part, people saw what they wanted to see. With any luck, whoever it was wouldn't head her way.

High heels clattered against the parquet floor. Whoever it was had chosen to wear heels despite the casual dress code. That made her curious. A quick peep took in classic navy pumps. As her eyes moved upward, passing over the telltale shininess of support pantyhose, a modest knee-length hemline, and up to a neat coiffure of silver-grey curls, she knew this was Barbie. This was no woman she could confuse with aimless chitchat.

The silver doors slid open, and the woman stepped onto the elevator. Della mentally counted to a hundred before moving. She stood slowly, uncertain that someone else might pop out. She should have noticed if there was someone there, but on the other hand, the woman hadn't noticed her, either. Cautiously, she eased out from behind the plants and strained her ears, listening for any sounds. A *click* followed by a *hiss* almost had Della jumping out of her flip flops until she recognized it as the heating system.

Get ahold of yourself. Time was wasting, and she needed to get in and get out. Della moved past the research area, knowing she'd find nothing there. Farther up, a narrow glass door fronted a small room with a utilitarian desk holding a computer, a potted plant, and a framed photo. It had to be Barbie's office. Beyond the small office, she could see another room with a bigger desk and a cushy desk chair.

35

That must be Lawson's office. It looked like there were no secrets between Lawson and his assistant. Since Barbie had left the office, Della expected it would be locked, but if miracles of all miracles happened and she'd forgotten to lock the door, the next door would surely be locked tight. Might as well try the door anyway.

Worried about leaving fingerprints, she pulled down her sleeve to cover her fingers. A modern forensic team could probably find her from a fiber residue left on the door. Still, they'd have no reason to call in a team since she intended to take nothing and leave the place the same as she found it. Her heartbeat sped up as she twisted the doorknob. What if she triggered an alarm?

The knob stayed solid, proving her initial suspicion that it would be locked, but the door moved slightly. Barbie must have locked the door and not pulled it closed all the way. How lucky was that? Using her shoulder, Della pushed the door open and slipped into the office.

If this were a movie, she'd boot up a computer and find the vital information simply by hacking the password in seconds. She heaved a sigh. Stupid idea, no real plan, and never mind she had made it to the top floor. Her gaze lingered on Barbie's desk. A small house plant, accompanied by a framed photo of smiling small children, possibly grandchildren, and a tiny gnome holding up a sign that said *Smile!* It all reminded Della of her mother's friend, Florence. Both women were possibly the same age.

Despite working for a software company, there was a good chance Barbie was like Florence. One thing she knew about Florence was she kept a datebook. While others consulted their phones for possible dates, Florence would always pull out her portable datebook. If Barbie had one, she might keep appointments for Lawson manually. As a bow to technology, she could transfer the information to an online calendar later.

A glance at her watch reminded her that in three minutes the guard would be on duty. It might be better if she were gone by that time. Della pulled two tissues from the box on the desk and used them to poke around the desk. Ironically, after pawing through paper clips, scissors, and cough drops, she found the daily planner on the desk top. The flowered agenda matched the blotter, causing it to blend into its surroundings.

Della carefully opened it, paging to a couple of weeks ago, and took a photo with her phone. She moved through the next couple of weeks and into the upcoming week. Jeffrey had a busy schedule. It made her wonder how many appointments he'd kept before disappearing. An elevator bell heralded someone coming up.

She froze as her eyes darted around the room. There was nowhere to hide in the glass panel office. The best she could do was wing it as a research person. Using her tissue, she pulled the door closed, making sure it caught. The elevator opened, and a blond man with a wispy mustache, garbed in a guard outfit exited, his tailored top pulling tight at his waistline. It wasn't just *any* guard!

"Hey, Della!"

Her eyes squeezed shut. "Hey, ah…" She tried hard to remember his name. There was no way she could pretend to be part of the research staff now. Could it get any worse? Their encounter had been the result of an ambush matchmaking. A former co-worker had invited Della to a dinner party a few months ago and had shamelessly sat her next to him at the table.

"Kyle," he told her. "It hasn't been all that long. Don't tell me you forgot!" He shot her a wide grin. "I'm surprised to see you up here. What are you doing on the twentieth floor?"

Oh my. She inhaled deeply, hoping for a reasonable excuse that would work with him and blurted out, "I'm the caterer for the McCormick/Lawson wedding. I've had some trouble getting some of the needed supplies for the canapes. I thought I'd come by and suggest a few alternatives."

"Makes sense," he accepted easily.

Most people would ask the bride or the mother of the bride, but she didn't point that out. She settled for an answering smile, which seemed to please him.

"I'll walk you out." Kyle gestured to the elevator. "It's policy, but I wouldn't mind renewing our acquaintance."

The last thing she wanted was for him to mention her upstairs visit. Any other woman might be able to flirt her way out of such a tight place. Flirting was so not her strong point, but she had to try. "I feel safer with you standing beside me." She managed a giggle that sounded strange even to her.

"You are safer."

The elevator doors opened. Inside, he stood much closer than needed in an elevator meant for at least a dozen people. This wasn't going in the direction she wanted.

"I feel so silly. I should have called the bride first. Could you not mention my visit? The bride can be a little fussy."

He chuckled. "That's not what *I* heard. Hear she was a real..." Kyle paused, realizing whatever he might have said would not have been appropriate. "Tell you what. I don't want you to get in trouble so I'm glad to help you out. Maybe we could go out sometime. That seems fair."

Not really, but Della knew she had to agree. "Sure. Come around the bakery and we can have coffee."

A ding preceded the elevator doors opening. Kyle gestured for Della to go first. "I work second shift, so I'll see you in the morning."

Della held her hand up to wave as she slipped into the garage. At least her mother would be pleased she had a date. Just maybe, she might have information about Lawson's disappearance, too.

CHAPTER FIVE

THE LATE AFTERNOON sun blinded Della as she pulled out of the Lawson Industries parking garage. Because of the extra time spent on her spying escapade, plus her chat time with Kyle, traffic had ballooned into a maddening snarl that jammed the city's narrow streets. The city of Owens had outgrown its infrastructure possibly fifty years ago which made it hard to get anywhere. This time of the day it wasn't too unusual to sit through a green traffic light because you couldn't move forward due to waiting vehicles.

A horn blared behind her. *Seriously?* Her rearview mirror revealed the driver of an oversized SUV to be the culprit, which meant the driver could see over her and could see there was no place to go. Still, the driver honked, possibly working out their frustrations but doing nothing for Della's. She blew out a breath that ruffled her bangs. What in the world might be happening at the bakery?

Even though her sluggish business caused her to go all James Bond on the missing bridegroom—minus the martinis, fast cars, beautiful girls, and gun—she hoped the daily rush had stayed slow.

The car in front of her crept forward but before she could do likewise, the light turned red, causing the honker to go back into full-out mode. Della imagined her car blowing out black smoke if only to annoy the driver. Maybe she could install a digital sign across her rear window that would alert drivers to her current state of mind—better not since she didn't want to alienate any potential customers.

When the light turned green, she goosed the gas pedal, causing the auto to jump—not a smooth move, but she did manage to get through the intersection. A downward glance revealed the temperature gauge creeping up into the hot section. She didn't need to deal with another issue.

"Come on, Betsy." Della had named her car a decade ago when she first got her.

Once she got to the bakery, the car could chill and cool off. She might even ask her mother to drop her off at her place. "Twelve, maybe thirteen more blocks, then you can rest. I'll get you premium if you just get me there."

It wasn't the first time she'd tried to bribe her car. For the most part, it worked since she kept chugging along. A wisp of steam undulated in front of her as if a dancer, hoping to gain attention, which it did. "Please, no."

At the last oil change, the mechanic had said something about her radiator, which she assumed was a way to pad the bill. It was just her luck to have an honest mechanic. Too bad she didn't listen to him.

There was no place for her to go unless she pulled into the parking lot of the beauty shop on her right. She exhaled audibly, knowing what she had to do.

THE BELL ON the bakery door jingled as Della pushed the door open. Her mother clutched a coffee cup and had her head down, watching something on her tablet—a sitcom by the sounds of the canned laughter. Since her mother failed to look up, Della opened the door again and closed it hard, making the bell dance for all its worth.

"Oh! There you are." Mabel gave her daughter a thorough once over. "Strange outfit for a customer service job."

Della's shoulders went up in a shrug. She didn't want to explain the thought that had gone into her useless disguise.

This didn't dissuade her mother much. "People today. No one bothers to dress for the job." A *tsking* sound punctuated the comment. "Anyhow, I was worried." Her eyes dropped to her tablet for a moment at an especially loud laugh-fest, then came back up. "I almost called the police."

"I'm glad you didn't." Della weaved her way through the tables, casually surveying the room. Every time she walked through the door, she tried to see the bakery the way your average customer might. She tweaked it daily to make it an inviting place. A bookcase on the far wall included books and board games. The second-hand books came from her personal library, with a few romances, courtesy of her mother. Some people did pick up a book to read, especially if they were alone. The board games were for use in the shop, which would make the customers stay longer. So far, no one had yet to open a game.

She ran her fingers through powdered sugar on a table. "This table is dirty."

"Oh that." Her mother shrugged and grimaced. "I ate over there. I'll clean it up." She disappeared behind the swinging door, returning with a wet cloth.

"Many customers?"

"Not really." Her mother gave the table a few half-hearted wipes, causing Della to press her lips together. Her mother had done so much to support her bakery she couldn't critique her table wiping. She could redo it later.

"How many?"

She held out one fisted hand, fingers up as she counted. She started over again. "Nine or more. I may have missed one or two during our courthouse fudge cookie rush. More importantly, Sexy and Bearded came back for a coffee refill. I'm pretty sure he was looking for you."

Every mother must believe their child is somehow better, smarter, or cuter than anyone else's child. In her mother's case, the woman went overboard with her belief that every man should be crazy not to be half in love with Della. *Should* was the operative word since the average guy tended to overlook her.

"I doubt it." Still, he was a private eye. Maybe he'd found out something. "Did he say anything about Lawson?"

Della moved behind the counter, sniffed the coffee, decided it was fresh enough, and poured herself a cup. She doctored it with hazelnut creamer and cinnamon.

Her mother pursed her lips. "Not sure. We talked about you, of course."

Della didn't even want to consider what her mother had said. Sometimes, total honesty via your mother was not the best way to make a good impression. "Anything else?"

"I told him about the speed dating event we're catering. Told him he should try it out. He could meet some nice women."

"Mom! Tell me no." She exhaled audibly. "Guys like him don't need speed dating." Della lifted the coffee cup to her lips as she recalled her mother's earlier words. "You told him we were catering the event. Why would you do that?"

"Because we are," her mother casually replied as she popped open the display case and picked out a cookie.

Della's mouth sputtered, spraying coffee onto the clean stainless-steel counter. After she finished coughing, she grabbed a napkin and wiped the counter. "What? When did this happen?"

"Oh…" Her mother drew out the word and smirked. "I don't just sit around waiting for folks to come in, you know. You're trying to patch up the McCormick/Lawson wedding, but I have doubts about that happening. With that in mind, we need to book some events around town. My friend Clarice knows the folks who oversee the after-five speed dating mixer. Since it's in a bar, they will have drinks, but no decent food. People need some finger foods they can carry around with them. It helps relieve the awkwardness. That way, if they get nothing else out of the experience, they'll have had some decent eats. You can leave your card out in case someone wants a catered event."

Wow! Leave her mother in charge and she was booking events. It made her wonder how her mother priced the event and what they expected for the price. "How much per plate? What are we serving?"

"I quoted them on French fried green beans, macaroni and cheese bites, fruit skewers, brownies, pigs in a blanket, pizza sticks, buffalo wings, and slaw."

"A little heavy."

"Maybe. The men will like it. Double up on the brownies for the women."

"Price?"

"Eleven dollars per person."

A little low, especially with the chicken wings and fruit skewers. Still, there would be a slight profit. "Makes me wonder how much they charge for this event that they can pay a caterer and still make money."

"Sixty dollars," Mabel stated before taking a bite of her cookie. She waved the cookie as she spoke. "A little high, but not too much if you meet the love of your life."

"I suppose." Della pulled out a chair and plopped into it. It wasn't the most comfortable seat, which might account for folks not staying overlong. Once they got out of the red, she really needed to upgrade the chairs. *Wait a minute.* She may be missing something. Being caught by Kyle, then basically hogtied into a coffee date, and having the car overheat, she wasn't as alert to her mother's machinations as usual.

It wasn't the first time her mother had mentioned speed dating, either, but when she did, it was to encourage Della to try it. "Um, Mom? You didn't sign me up for the speed dating, did you?"

Mabel arched her eyebrows and wrinkled her nose. "How do you think I sealed the deal? None of the other caterers were willing to sign up."

"They were probably married."

"All the same, you've got to make your own opportunities. Don't worry about serving. It's a buffet. Clarice promised to help because I'll be one of the contestants, too." She shimmied her shoulders and laughed.

The men of Owens wouldn't know what hit them. Sure, she'd told her mother several times she should give dating a try. Della could remember her mom fussing over her dad from his clothes to fixing his favorite dishes, always happiest doing for others. There had to be lots of widowers or even single men who would be up for that kind of treatment. Still, they'd have to pass Della's inspection.

As for her mother signing up, that was to pacify Della. Her mother would probably make sure to edge her way in front of her daughter so she could do public relations for Della before arriving at each table.

Della's friend Kelly had tried speed dating. She told her each participant had less than five minutes to make a good impression, which might have worked for her friend, who was a deejay and knew how to create the right image.

Five minutes could be a lifetime in a car spinning out of control on a rain-slicked highway, but it would be barely long enough to cover hellos and mutual excuses of why they chose speed-dating. Once she admitted her mother had signed her up, any man would think she lived in her parents' basement. Those who wouldn't be creeped out were probably driven there by their own parents.

"Mom!"

"No need to thank me. I paid for it myself. Nothing is too good for my daughter. I want you to have the best."

A cruise, a new car, even a spa day would be the best, not speed dating. Her mother had such a pleased expression, certain she had done something wonderful. In her eyes, she had. Her parents had shared a loving relationship, and it was natural her mother wanted the same for her. Never mind that things today were entirely different. Women didn't meet their future husband in high school, marry, have children, and live happily ever after. Modern women wanted something more, such as a career.

"Thanks." Once she got to the place, she'd explain to the host that she had no intention of participating and they could keep the money anyway. Who would argue with that? Everyone knew there were always more women than men at these things. One less woman would even things up. "I did find out a little at the temp job. By the way, I'm going back tomorrow, which means I must be in here all the earlier to bake. You get anything from your gossip hotline?"

Her mother groaned. "I did try. Apparently, anyone who has had the misfortune to encounter Ellie McCormick thinks she's a gold digger who has somehow bewitched that nice Jeffrey Lawson. Prevailing gossip is theirs is no great love affair. Turns out Ellie got dumped by another guy about the time she latched onto Lawson. Rumor is she'd told everyone about the previous guy and how he was about to pop the question. I think Mildred told me he was a sports car driver and drove the NASCAR circuit or something. The question he popped must have been more like, will you just leave me alone?"

"That would sting. Lawson is the most eligible bachelor around. So naturally, she set her sights on him. It would make her unofficial royalty in town. I don't get what Lawson sees in her outside of her luxurious mane of hair, perfect skin, blinding white smile, and enviable figure."

"Men." Her mother sniffed. "Even the smart ones can turn up dumb when a pretty girl is on the scene."

Once, she had been engaged in casual chit-chat with a fellow baker at a restaurant showcase. When a female like Ellie walked by, the man stopped in mid-sentence, following the woman as if caught in her orbit.

"I hear you." She shook her head with remembered disgust and aggravation. "From my short time at Lawson Industries today, the Lawson family can be penny pinchers about some things. We had an old school clock in the customer service area. I'd swear it was from my old grade school. Then there were the chairs." Her hand crept back to her lower back. "No lumbar support at all. They may have been as old as the clock. Don't think money is going to flow as freely as Ellie might think. Do you remember Ellie casually mentioning they'd be serving lamb at the rehearsal dinner and her fiancé corrected her?"

Her mother laughed. "Glad I was there to hear him say, 'Chicken is good enough for both our families. If they want lamb, they can head to a Mediterranean restaurant.'"

"Yeah. I bet you mentioned that tidbit to a few of your friends."

Her mother polished off the cookie and then held up her index finger. "Only a few. I told them it was on the QT."

That meant most of the town knew. She hoped Ellie couldn't trace it back to her, but chances were she might assume her fiancé was the culprit. No one would come right out and laugh in Ellie's face about the chicken being good enough comment. That would just be rude and more like something Ellie would do. "I need this wedding, but more and more I find myself feeling sorry for Jeffrey Lawson."

"He's a grown man who runs an international company. Surely he can handle one woman."

"You'd think. Let me show you what I got, then I'll have to make up some batter and put it into the fridge to chill." Della reached into her bag and felt around until she found the rectangular shape of her phone and withdrew it. She thumbed open the gallery and enlarged the images of the datebook. She squinted at the squiggles on the page—they made no sense to her. Sometimes, they were letters and other times, just a symbol or two written beside a time.

"What else can go wrong today?" She fashioned her forefinger and thumb into a gun and mimed shooting herself.

"Oh, Della. Quit being so dramatic. Let me see."

Her mother strolled over to Della and peered at the phone, letting her daughter babble on. "I roped myself into a coffee date with the guard for this."

"Oh really?" Her mother raised her eyebrows and then reached into her shirt and pulled out her readers. "Ah, it's shorthand."

An old school secretary would use shorthand. Maybe she was afraid certain chefs might be peering into her datebook. "You know shorthand?"

"A little. I used to be a secretary before I married your father."

Della's mouth fell open. Her mother had never mentioned that. She assumed her mother had married out of high school. It made her wonder what else she didn't know. "You never told me that."

"No reason to do so. I would have if you'd asked."

There was no real scenario Della could think of where she'd ask her mother if she had been a secretary. "Can you read it?"

Her eyes went back and forth, then her lips pulled down. "Not really. This could be vital information. We need someone who's good at shorthand and still uses it to take notes."

It sounded like a build-up to Della, but she still asked. "You know someone like that?"

"Well, yes, I do. We went to secretarial school together. She was the best at dictation. I, on the other hand, could type."

Because the intro lasted longer than her mother's usual ones, it made her a tad anxious. "Tell me. I've got batter to make."

"Clarice."

A groan sounded, which Della assumed must have come from her. After all, why wouldn't they want to consult with her mother's best friend and the biggest gossip in town?

CHAPTER SIX

ORNING HIT DELLA like an anvil dropped by a persistent coyote. Unlike the cartoon roadrunner, she didn't make a cocky reply and speed away. Instead, she stared at her ceiling while the alarm chirped in her right ear. Four-thirty and time to roll out of bed. It didn't matter if she didn't want to get up. Still, as an adult, she needed to act like one.

Her feet hit the cold floor as she forced herself to stumble through the dark apartment. It would have been easier if she'd lived over the bakery, but that unit had been snagged by a renter twenty years ago who had no desire to move. Instead, Della moved into an aging apartment complex with faded wood shingles and out-of-control shrubbery.

Night lights lit her way. Bakers had to arrive before dawn to make all the fresh goodies. Didn't mean she had to like it or assault her eyes with bright light until the last moment. Preparing to leave, she took a quick glance into the mirror to make sure she didn't resemble something seen on a late-night horror flick.

At the bakery, she could grab coffee and breakfast. If time allowed, she could even duck into the bathroom to slap on some makeup or attempt to rearrange her hair onto some sort of style. Normally, her hair was covered by a disposable hat for hygiene purposes. The result was extreme hat hair with her hair flattened down on all sides. Some water and tousling made it a little less yucky. She wiggled into a pair of chef pants and considered briefly wearing them to her temp position but discarded the idea as quickly as she came up with it.

Starting a business gobbled up money like a marathon runner carbo-loading the night before the race. The extra money the temp position provided was a godsend. Khaki pants and a polo shirt went into her tote bag, along with a few toiletries. She added a hairbrush and wondered if she should add earrings since Kyle might show up. Della shook her head hard. "Wake up! This is Kyle we're talking about." She wasn't crazy about him at the ambush dinner, and she wasn't crazy about him now.

If she remembered correctly, he spent most of his time talking about his fantasy football league. Many people ramble when nervous. It was hard to remember what nonsense she had mumbled after she realized she'd been the victim of a match-up, again. Married couples and those in a relationship had issues with just inviting single friends over to watch a movie or for game night. Since they had paired up, they assumed everyone needed to do likewise. Maybe it made the amateur matchmakers feel better, imagining themselves bringing romantic bliss to their single friends.

Next, she donned her chef's smock, the symbol of her trade. It took her almost four years to earn the culinary arts degree, splitting her time between working at her mortgage company job and taking an online course. Even though her school had trumpeted that Della could earn her degree online, she'd had her doubts. Puttering around in her own kitchen and submitting photos of her creations wasn't the same as watching someone bite into her pumpkin butterscotch muffin. A word from her chatty mother in the right ear helped her land an internship at a popular bakery, Baby Cakes, in the nearby town of Centerville. Even though her online school didn't have an actual graduation, the employees at Baby Cakes put together a ceremony, including presenting her with her official chef coat.

If Kyle showed up before she took off for her temp job, he'd have to take her as she was. No squeezing into shapewear and packing on makeup. If he preferred a glossy beauty, he wouldn't have pressed to meet again.

Her backpack loaded, she turned to leave and placed her hand on the door, only to remember her car was not outside but in front of the bakery earning a well-deserved rest. Not driving didn't guarantee it would repair itself, but it had worked before. Her lips pressed together as she considered her next action. At one point, she considered herself lucky to live so close to the bakery. That assumption relied on driving almost three miles.

Her mother had dropped her off the night before and commented she'd come back to pick her up in the morning. Della couldn't remember if she'd agreed, exhausted from working two jobs. Her mother might have told her she'd sign her up for a mission to Mars, and Della would have muttered, "That's nice."

It was too early for any car services to be cruising around the town. Owens' small population didn't rate a taxi service. There was no help for it. She'd have to walk, which would cut into her baking time. Della pulled the door shut and checked the lock before jogging down the stairs. The chilly air penetrated her chef smock, making her rethink her decision to forgo a jacket. Her pace increased, pumping blood to her extremities, and warming her up.

The hum of a car motor accompanied by headlights had her taking a tighter grip on her backpack and breaking into a jog/walk.

There was no reason to break into a full run and signal her trepidation. Normally, Owens's crime spree consisted of high school senior stealing the anatomy skeleton from the school and sending photos to the school of the skeleton partying in various places. After a few weeks, the culprits grew tired of their shenanigans and left Mr. Bones in a public place with a note to return him back to school. In a twisted way it served as a rite of passage for the soon-to-be graduates.

Still, her heart skipped, remembering all the true-crime dramas she favored. The show always started with towns not too unlike her own, places where people left their doors unlocked, although that only happened when she forgot. It just meant Owens could be ripe for a major crime. Why else would they hire guards for Logan Industries? Sweat pebbled Della's upper lip and forehead despite the brisk temps. Her gut told her not to look, but she still peeked behind her, figuring it might give her a jump on the situation. The square headlights looked vaguely familiar.

An electronic buzz of a window going down vibrated through the heavy stillness, then a voice. "Della, get in the car!"

How did the driver know her name? It took a few seconds. "Mom! What are you doing here?"

She waited until her mother braked before taking hold of the door, opening it, and climbing inside. After she slammed the door, her mother roared off, grumbling a little as she did so. "I can't believe you were going to try to walk to the bakery. We discussed this last night. Did you think I'd forget to get you? Set my alarm the minute I got home."

Elephants might be famous for not forgetting, but they couldn't hold a candle to Mabel Delacroix. "It's not you. I was so tired last night I had no clue what I said. Even forgot you dropped me off until I got ready to leave."

"Poor dear. You were pretty much dead on your feet. A gal isn't meant to burn a candle at both ends. What you need…"

Before her mother could finish her sentence, the car bumped up over a curb, hit the ground with a jolt, hardly slowing down, and provided the break Della needed from the popular refrain about how a husband would take care of her. In her mother's world, there must be a store that stocked available men for matrimonial purposes. It was best to distract her before she went back to the uncomfortable topic. "You probably ran over the azalea bushes the groundskeeper just planted. I think it was management's idea of upgrading the place to attract more renters."

"The groundskeeper shouldn't put it somewhere it would get run over." Her mother glibly said the words, possibly believing them as her right hand drifted to the console. The car swerved slightly as Mabel glanced in the direction of her right hand.

"Mother!" Della chose that moment to buckle her seatbelt. "What do you need? I'll find it for you."

"You nervous or something?"

"Just trying to help." Even though the words were pushed out through a clenched jaw, they were true nonetheless. Della should be used to her mother's driving because it wasn't something that gradually got better. Her father used to tease his wife about driving too fast. Apparently, her mother took the statement either as a compliment or a dare. Since no major accidents had resulted, nothing changed.

"Sweetie," her mother started, "I've been thinking."

Della squeezed her eyes shut, wishing she was back in bed but opened them again. Nothing good ever came from starting with *I've been thinking*. It was up there with *we need to talk*. Since she doubted her mother would be disowning her, she had no clue what could be up.

A car headed toward them but swerved onto the shoulder as it passed them. Mom did love to hug the middle line. Once the car passed, Della let out a breath. "Okay. What have you been thinking?"

"You need a companion."

"Mom." Too early and she hadn't had any coffee.

"Hear me out. I'm not talking the two-legged kind. A pet. You had several pets growing up and loved them all."

All through her childhood, a furry companion of some sort listened to her problems. At that time, she thought not making the field hockey team ranked as a major deal. "True. I imagined a cat in the bakery. It would make the place more inviting, but the board of health would shut us down. Too bad, though. I liked the idea of a cat."

"How about a puppy?" her mother suggested in a leading manner.

"Why do you ask?" Mabel would make a better sleuth than she did. Not only did she have an excellent memory, but she also kept moving odd bits of information around until they made a connection. Della knew that for a fact. She was used to having her mother grill her with random questions that allowed her guard to drop before going in with the zinger. At least she'd eased off the what-you-need-is-a-husband angle. Her urge to see Della wed made its appearance after her father's unexpected death. Going with Cupid's Catering Company as a name seemed to inspire her mother to see who she could pair off.

"Oh…" Mabel stretched out the word as she slowed for a stop. "I saw an ad in the paper for puppies. I thought how sweet it would be to have one."

As much as she loved her former pets, Della remembered the work. Unlike many parents who took over when their child dropped the pet-care ball, hers didn't. Instead, they reminded her daily about her duties, often inserting a mini lecture on responsibility. "I think that would be a great idea for *you*. Pets take a great deal of work."

Her mother chuckled. "I know. That's why I thought we could own it together."

"I'm not sure what you're getting at. Wouldn't it be confusing for the animal? It would be like we had joint custody. I'm much too busy for a pet."

"Hmmm…" Mabel murmured her response, which was no response at all. "Maybe you should take my car. After all, I'll be at the bakery which means I won't be going anywhere."

That should keep the residents of Owens safe for a few hours. "Sure. That's awfully generous of you."

"That's what mothers do." She managed to squeeze a little more speed from the sedan to scoot through a light turning red. "I might even give Horace a call. You remember? He worked on my car before."

She remembered. Her father used to joke that Mabel had a more serious relationship with the mechanic than with her own husband. One of the reasons could have been Horace did bodywork, too. A person couldn't drive as if her car were a Sherman tank and not expect a little damage. Mabel blamed the dings and scratches on parking lot offenders, which *could* have happened.

The street lights and a handful of glowing neon signs illuminated downtown. Even though a lit shop provided security against burglars, Della made do with a couple of table lamps with low wattage bulbs to do the job. It saved on electricity and provided a cozy ambiance.

"We're here," Della said unnecessarily.

"Time to make the donuts," her mother quipped back, quoting a long-ago commercial.

"Donuts. I never considered that." It just might be the stopper that would plug the fast flow of money from her hands into her supplier's hands. First, she'd have to investigate the competition. No problem there. She might be able to squeeze a few minutes between getting food ready for speed date mixer, her temp job, and finding the Lawson heir.

CHAPTER SEVEN

DELLA TAPPED THE side of the small sifter filled with confection-ery sugar. A sweet cloud drifted onto the still-warm pumpkin muffins. Metal clanking on metal signaled Mabel assembling the enormous coffee urn. The one thing Cupid Catering Company sold a great deal of coffee. Fast food restaurants, coffee shops, and gas stations sold coffee, which meant hers had to be better to make someone abandon the convenience of a drive thru. No one sold Della's special blend, which came from mixing two separate types of java together and adding a few select spices.

"Would you like to take over here while I blend the coffee?"

Her mother gave her an eye slant but took the offered sifter. "I know you don't want me to know your special blend. While I *do* gossip, I'd never give away your trade secrets. However, you might need me to know. What if I run out while you're gone?"

I know you wouldn't, she thought, but said, "I'll make up some extra and put it in a container by the urn for you. When is Clarice coming by?"

"About six-thirty-ish. Her shift at the hospital starts at seven. I told her there wasn't a great deal to translate, just a few random words." Her mother held up her hand as if to stop whatever Della might say. It happened to be the hand holding the sifter full of confectionery sugar, which dusted the floor instead of the sweet treats.

Her mother's crestfallen face made it impossible to be too upset. Cooks in fancy restaurants used to wear wooden clogs to keep from slipping on whatever dropped on the floor, be it eggs, vegetable oil, or confectionary sugar. Traditions probably changed with the inventions of non-slip shoes with arch support.

"No worries. I'll let you clean it up after we get everything ready."

"Thanks." Her mother put her free hand on her hip and wrinkled her nose. "If you have time, you need to get the supply list together for what we need for the mixer. You can send it to me from work or call it in on your lunch hour."

Della carefully measured the French roast coffee into the oversized glass measuring cup she used for mixing. "Ah yeah. Will do. How many people do they have signed up?"

"Sixty-three. Make sure to add in the organizers because they will be sure to pick up a plate. There might be a couple of walk-ins, too. Seventy might be a better bet. Some will eat out of nervousness."

"I'd better make more, then." The thought furrowed her brow. Catering, while it did feed people and made life easier for the host, needed to be profitable for the caterer. "I didn't think we even had that many eligible men in Owens."

"Nah. I'd stay at seventy. Plenty of women won't eat anything, afraid they might be judged on how they ate. The menu isn't exactly finger sandwiches and tea. I can imagine the more genteel females prying the fruit from skewers with a fork, unlike their male counterparts who'll either pluck it off with their fingers or bite it directly off the stick."

"Bowls would be helpful, then. I'll put half the fruit on skewers and the rest in bowls. It's the least I can do to help someone make their love connection." She laughed, realizing how she sounded. "Oh my. I sound just like you."

An oven buzzer chimed, triggering Mabel to don oven mitts. "You say it like it's a bad thing."

The two of them got the coffee going and the display case filled before Clarice arrived in her turquoise nursing scrubs and full makeup. She tapped on the still locked door. Mabel stopped what she was doing and rushed to open the door for her friend.

The middle-aged woman strolled in. The heavy blusher on Clarice's face announced her refusal to move out of the 80s era and opt for subtler enhancements. She gave the air an appreciative sniff and plopped her oversized purse on the counter. "I could use some coffee with cream and a pumpkin muffin."

Della knew Clarice well enough to know the woman wouldn't pay, but if she could figure out the incomprehensible shorthand, she'd load her up with muffins and possibly a brownie, too. She bustled to collect the requested items and made a stop at her purse to retrieve the printout of the datebook. The whole affair was rather clandestine, but to shove a phone in front of Clarice's face and ask her opinion somehow felt off. She'd enlarged the images before she printed them just in case there was a reading issue.

The coffee cup made a slight tap as she placed it on the table first, allowing Clarice to take a sip before she put the muffin on the table with a napkin-wrapped fork. Finally, she unfolded the papers. A simple nod had her mother bringing a full coffee cup and a pen to join her friend.

Even though Della wanted to be right there, she knew her mother would get more out of her friend. Mabel also understood Clarice's cryptic comments due to their decades of friendship. Della would have to stop and ask for an explanation. With her luck, Clarice could get mad and leave without finishing the datebook.

The bell above the door jingled as it admitted two thirty-something women. One yawned while the other smiled in her direction and spoke. "I heard you had the best coffee around."

"Of course, we do. Would you like a sample?"

Her mother pushed back her chair hard, making it squeak. Della got her parent's eye and received a hard head shake. Yep, she did it again. Sometimes she blamed being in the red on lack of customers, but part of it was on her, too. When she did have customers, she offered them free samples. Many filled up on the samples and left with a plain coffee or sometimes, nothing at all.

The customer in question waved off the sample and extracted a thermos cup from her handbag. "Fill this up, please. Do you have some program where if you buy five coffees, you get one free?"

"I could. Hadn't considered it until now. When you return, I'll have a punch card for you with one hole already punched."

The woman beamed up and nudged her friend. "Good deal."

After some discussion, the women left with scones and a blueberry muffin along with their coffee. Once the door closed, Della picked up a damp cloth to wipe already clean tables to see how things were going.

Her mother wrote slowly as she repeated back the word. "Bardstown."

"That's what I said. Weird. I imagine it's a place, but it could be a name. Why do you need me to do this?"

Unfortunately, they hadn't worked out a cover story. Mabel coughed once, then mumbled "Top secret."

"Oh…" Clarice lengthened the word. "I get it. You're trying to out a cheater. It sure would have been nice if he had put more details in his daybook, such as flying to the Bahamas with my latest bimbo."

Della must have moved a trifle too close because Clarice glanced up and held up one finger. "I heard you signed up for speed dating."

She hadn't, but she did appreciate the business her mother's friend threw their way. "I do appreciate the opportunity to cater."

"Yeah, cater." She nodded her head. "Plenty of men would be gaga about you since you can cook, but be careful. I heard some of the men who sign up for speed dating are already in relationships. I guess they want to test the waters to see what's still out there." She pointed to the datebook papers. "Like this cheater here."

Even though Della didn't know Jeffrey Lawson that well, he didn't strike her as a player. "I'll be careful." What had she gotten herself into? She planned to take refuge behind the buffet table.

The bell jingled again. This was more business than they usually got this time of day. Ethan Stone sauntered in, looking like an ad for some adventure magazine in his peacoat with a plaid scarf draped around his neck.

"Coffee, black?" she asked.

He fashioned his thumb and forefinger into a gun shape and pointed it at her. "Right on target. I'm under your spell."

Did he say he was under her spell? Since she'd never been a sultry beauty, no one ever claimed to be bewitched or under her spell. It made no sense but pleased her all the same. Della grinned at the man as he spoke.

"Coffee. Your coffee keeps me coming back, plus the cookies have a magnetic pull."

Her unexpected elation deflated rather like a subpar bounce

house. He was under the spell of her coffee and cookies. Why had she thought otherwise?

"What size coffee? Check out the pumpkin muffins. They should still be warm from the oven."

His eyes drifted to the display over her head showing the different size cups with their names. She had taken a cue from a famous coffee shop and gave the sizes cute names. His eyes moved back and forth as he read, and his lips tilted up in a smile. "I'm going to need the T-Rex today. I'll take two pumpkin muffins."

Della poured his coffee and handed it to him. If it was his first cup of the day, he'd want it yesterday. She started to bag the muffins, but turned to ask, "To go?"

"No, here. I thought we could talk about your new job at Lawson Industries."

Boy, he *was* good. She wondered how he'd found out she took a temp position. Oh yeah, her mother. She plated the muffins and added the napkin-wrapped fork. "Six dollars and thirty-five cents."

Ethan held her gaze as he paid. A tiny flicker of amusement danced in his eyes. Did her aggravation over his knowing more about her life than he should show? She couldn't blame him when her mother so freely gave information. She could refuse to sit with him. Not only would that be rude, but her mother happened to be right about him being both interesting and sexy.

She grabbed a cup of coffee and her own muffin. It would keep her hands busy and not betray her nervousness. One of the other reasons she kept away from Clarice was she couldn't fabricate convincingly. Her mother used to tease her about her face betraying her whenever she lied. She said she looked like she'd eaten too many green apples, a tidbit not revealed until after Della's teen years.

Maybe Ethan wouldn't ask her anything that would be fib worthy. He already knew she worked at Lawson Industries. No reason to ask if she'd attempted to break into the CEO's office while pretending to be a research and development assistant.

The conversation started out pleasantly with Ethan complimenting her muffin and asking her about why she wanted to be a baker. Della knew from watching old Columbo shows that this was how the investigator disarmed the suspect by asking about something mundane, yet personal. The bell jingled when she reached the part of her story where she baked her own cookies for the elementary school bake sale.

Another customer. Her head jerked up in time to witness Kyle entering the bakery. She had totally forgotten about their coffee date. Even though they agreed to meet today, she assumed it wasn't happening. People say let's do lunch or grab a drink with no intention to act on it. Della half-raised in her chair, ready to move behind the counter when Kyle spotted her.

The pleasant, down-to-earth guy she met yesterday morphed before her very eyes. His face reddened or maybe it was already flushed due to being outdoors. His chin went up, and Della would have sworn his nostrils flared, but that only happened with cartoon characters. His gloved hands did clench into fists.

"I thought we had a coffee date." He growled the words, earning a censorious look from Mabel with Clarice settling for a sniff to signal her disapproval.

Ethan jumped to his feet. "You need to stand down."

This was not what she needed this morning. She moved behind the counter, feeling safer with the barrier between them. "We did have a coffee date. Let me get you some coffee."

Part of her wanted to throw it on him, but that wouldn't help. He'd probably pull some strings and get her fired. Temps didn't have job security. It would be her only chance of pumping her workmates about the information Clarice deciphered.

Kyle gave Ethan a dirty look before advancing toward the counter, bringing with him the smell of the outdoors and cigarette smoke. He gave her a short nod and audibly exhaled. "My bad. I guess I overreacted. My girlfriend left me over a pretty boy like him. They come in with their smooth lines and polished manners, saying everything a woman wants to hear. I saw you there and went ballistic. Brother?"

She couldn't confirm his hopeful inquiry since she wouldn't lie.

Mabel and Ethan had no trouble since they both said "Cousin" at the same time and shot each other puzzled looks.

Kyle turned to Ethan and said, "Sorry. You know how it is."

Instead of replying, Ethan saluted him with his coffee cup.

Della brandished a coffee cup and asked, "How do you like your coffee?"

"Seven sugars, heavy cream, and a dash of cinnamon."

Well, that explained his quick temper. His blood must be half sugar. She made his coffee and handed it to him. "See anything in the display case that looks good to you?"

"Now, if you asked me about behind the counter..." he drawled.

Do not roll your eyes. A quick pivot put her in front of the display case, hiding any betraying emotions her face might make. Even though she blamed her lack of popularity on not being a conventional beauty, her plain talk and not hiding her emotions could have played a part in it. With her back turned to Kyle she asked, "Muffin? Cookie? Scone?"

"Yeah," he replied, not differentiating what he wanted. Della piled all three on a plate and passed it to him. He'd expect her to sit with him since most people tended to do that on a date. She moved slowly around the counter, aware she had three eavesdroppers nearby. All she had to do was make small talk, then mention she had to get ready for work. Since it was the truth, her face wouldn't betray her.

Della led the way to a table the farthest away. It couldn't have been more than eight feet at the most. The ovens, prep area, and walk-in freezer reigned over most of the shop, leaving a minuscule dining area. "Here we are."

She perched on the edge of her chair, ready to jump up if a customer entered. Her initial impressions and memories from the impromptu dinner party washed over. Sure, he had yammered on about his fantasy football league. That wasn't what turned her off, though. Kyle launched into a full rundown of how his previous girlfriend did him wrong. Why he even mentioned it baffled her. No woman wanted to hear about another woman on her date. Even worse, by badmouthing his ex, it just made him look bad.

While most men may have thought trash talking their previous girlfriend would somehow vindicate them, it didn't. It waved flags like a landing signal officer on a busy aircraft carrier. Instead, women tended to identify with the absent woman, wondering how she'd explain their relationship and subsequent break-up.

Della managed to make sympathetic noises while estimating how many chicken wings she should order. She usually used the same distributor, but she had a significant coupon for a different one. Should she take a chance? *Wait a minute.* Kyle had stopped talking.

"Pardon me?"

"I said Lawson Industries was broken into last night."

Della almost said, that was me. Instead, she asked, "When?"

"Ten-thirty-five pm. I was in the garage when the alarm sounded."

The breath she'd taken and held, slowly released. Good. It wasn't her. Kyle could have been on a smoke break. "Was anything taken?"

He shook his head. "I don't know. I just follow the protocol. Whoever it was vanished by the time I reached the top floor, but Mr. Lawson's office was open, so I called the police. They fingerprinted the area."

Thank goodness she had pulled her chef smock over her hands. A top-notch forensic team would be able to pick up fibers from her smock, identify it, and pin down what brand it was. At least, they could on all the cold case shows.

Kyle cleared his throat and stood. "Della, could you introduce me to your cousin? It would give me another chance at making a good impression on your family."

Della blinked before remembering her connection to Cousin Ethan. In her opinion, good impressions left about the time he arrived. What else could happen?

Clarice's voice shattered the short silence. "I'd love to stay, but since I'm the shift head, I've got to leave. I've already overstayed my time, and I'll have to put me on report for being late."

Mabel waved her off and the doorbell jingle signaled Clarice's departure.

Even though it was the last thing she wanted to do, Della stood and angled her head at her coffee date. "Kyle, meet Ethan."

She didn't trust herself to say the word cousin. Kyle thrust out his hand in greeting, which Ethan took. The two testing each other's firmness of handshake provided an opportunity to drift back to the kitchen where her mother was already holding the deciphered pages.

"Anything?"

"Depends." Her mother blew out a breath. "We have the words Logistics, Bardstown, Stephanie, Norris Pointe, and Downtown Imports."

An odd assortment of words. "I'd be willing to bet the Imports have something to do with his car or maybe plans to get a new one."

"That's what I thought," her mother agreed, and then tapped the side of her nose. "You need to find out what type of car he has."

"True. On that note, I need to get changed. I must say the name Stephanie intrigues me the most."

"Me, too."

The clatter of a chair falling came from the front. When Della started toward the door, her mother grabbed her arm and pointed to the bathroom. "Go get ready. You can take my car. Remember to fill it up. I've got this." She gestured to the front of the store.

Even though Della liked to think of herself as a can-do gal, she'd let her mother handle this one. Who knows? The men could be wrestling for all she knew. The male species could be odd at times in their effort to show off for other guys. Her mother would be the best one to stop them. Before her mother's retirement, she used to teach science at a school for wayward boys. Mabel had probably lost count of how many fights she'd stopped.

Della needed to get to work and find out who Stephanie was and Lawson's car model. Just maybe she'd find out about Bardstown, Logistics, and Norris Point if she could figure out how to work the words into a casual conversation.

CHAPTER EIGHT

I NSIDE THE CUSTOMER Support Advantage cubicle, conversations twisted and mingled in the air while other lines constantly buzzed with irate customers. Della inhaled before pushing the button to take the next call. If the individual on the other end wasn't angry when they first called, after listening to tinny hold music forever, they were when she answered.

Forcing her lips into a smile, she said, "Welcome to Lawson Customer Advantage hotline."

What a misnomer. It made it sound like the customer could connect with the needed help. It didn't take her long to realize people just wanted to complain. Usually, after a hard ranting of five to eight minutes, they calmed down enough for her to transfer them. A few went into the state of the world since they were already in rant mode. Unfortunately, this happened to be one of those calls.

Todd drifted in and smirked at the busy customer service repre- sentatives. He rubbed his hands together. "I've got some juicy gossip about the break-in."

Even though there had been a legitimate break-in, Della still swallowed hard. Her fingerprints might not be on the doors, but it could be on the plant or elevator button. Kyle saw her there, too.

A lull in the customer conversation allowed her to insert, "I'm so sorry to hear that. You didn't deserve that. How can I help you?"

Her finger hovered over the tech button when the woman said, "Oh, I'm fine now. I appreciate your listening. You're a real sweetheart. My son just arrived, and he's going to look at it."

"So glad to hear that. Have a nice day." This was one time the required sign off that informed the frustrated caller to have a nice day didn't throw gasoline on the fire.

"I will, sweetie. You, too."

"Thank you. I will."

That is, if I don't get arrested. She hung up, ignored the buzzing lines, and pivoted her chair to face her gossiping co-workers. Della arched her brows, unsure if she should even ask. Would a temp be that interested in what happened in a company she had no investment in? On the crime shows, either a criminal was obvious because they didn't ask since they knew all the details already, or their apparent interest caused suspicions. Her teeth bit down on her bottom lip. No matter what she did it could make her look guilty.

Lori must have witnessed her curiosity and took pity on her. She wrapped a casual arm around Todd. "Our own gossip gatherer has brought us a tale of a break-in last night. No one was caught, but the police were brought in. Word is the security system was bypassed, which means it was an inside job."

Goodness! That did sound like her. "What did they steal?"

Todd fielded the question. "It would be easy if a computer or a printer was gone, but actually, nothing physical is missing."

Before he could continue, Lori glanced side to side as if afraid someone might be listening. "It had to be information."

"Information?" Della echoed the words, wondering what the intruder wanted. For all she knew, it could be Ethan Stone trying to locate Jeffrey Lawson. Knowing Ethan, he had better luck than her.

"Yep," Todd hurried to assure everyone before Lori stole his story. "I heard it from IT. Once they heard about the break-in, they started checking the last time various computers had been accessed."

Good thing she hadn't even tried to power up Barbie's computer. "Did they find something?"

Todd placed a finger to his lips, which caused the others to move closer, even Della who used her feet to pull her chair closer. Seeing he had his audience in close, he continued. "I heard the big guy's computer was booted up."

"What did they get?" Jaime asked.

The fact she'd ask meant the woman was as curious as Della.

Their informant grew quiet and sighed heavily. "That's when the IT guys noticed me and quit talking. I was bringing them coffee."

What in the world could be happening? The news of an actual break-in, as opposed to her little look-see, created new motivations for Lawson's disappearance. On the way to work, the idea of an old flame named Stephanie seemed like a reasonable excuse for Lawson missing work. Having worked with Bridezilla, she'd formed an unlikely scenario where his guy friends whisked him away to an isolated cabin to deprogram him before the marriage.

"Sounds like a movie," Jaime remarked and nodded to each person. She raised her right hand above her head and dangled her fingers in the air. "Makes me wonder if they dropped from the ceiling." Her hand dropped to waist level.

Lori, who dropped her arm from Todd's shoulder, gave her co-worker a thumbs up. "I bet they downloaded all the information on the computer onto a thumb drive and got away with it."

Their supervisor, who had listened to all the speculation, cleared her throat. "We need to get back to work." She held up one finger.

"You do know the entire top floor is composed of glass. It was a peculiarity of the older Lawson. Claimed he had the best view in the city." Tyesha coughed. "It's not like Owens is Rome or anything. Anyhow, no one could drop in without shattering the ceiling. If someone was digging into Lawson's computer, they'd be sadly disappointed. None of the Lawsons design the software. Maybe they did once, but that's all research and development now"

Cogs turned as Della listened. Lawson Industries employed software engineers who could be the real brains behind the scene, which meant the Lawson family mainly handled marketing and sales. They were the face of the company. What if someone grabbed him? It could be a dissatisfied customer who meant to bring the man home to fix their tech issues. That idea sounded farfetched even to herself. Some folks might think it could be a kidnapping for hire, but as far as she knew, no ransom had been demanded. Then, who had hired Ethan Stone? He certainly had never mentioned that pertinent information.

A hand landing on her shoulder startled Della. Hairs stood up on her arms as a tiny moment of terror grabbed her. The casual touch reminded her how easily Lawson could have been grabbed. Tyesha gave her an odd look, then dropped her hand. "You need to get back to work. It looks like you drifted off to dreamland. Thinking of your boyfriend?"

"No." Her cheeks heated as she stood and pushed her chair back to her station. "I don't have a boyfriend."

Tyesha angled up her chin. "That's not what I hear." She turned on her heel and vanished into her office.

What she meant didn't sound like anything Della wanted to delve into. She probably would not like what she found.

AFTER LISTENING TO several irate customers, she wondered if Lawson's products were any good at all. If the program worked, why all the calls? Once she noticed Jaime was off the phone, she sauntered by her cubicle. In less than twenty-four hours, she decided Jaime would deliver facts without any pokes back about why she asked. She slowed, stopped at Jaime's cubicle, and waited for her to notice.

The customer rep glanced over her shoulder, then swiveled her seat. "Hey, Della. Having a problem with a caller?"

"Not really." Her shoulders went up in a shrug. "I was wondering what software Lawson markets, and why do we get so many irate calls complaining about them?"

"Ever notice the callers never say what *isn't* working with their software?"

Most of the callers insisted the software didn't work and remarked it wasn't like the commercials. Nothing was ever like the commercials, but Della managed to keep that thought to herself. One swore it must have been designed by someone who wanted people to remain single. A few grumbled about it being impossible to use. Some might ask if it was improperly installed or possibly broken, which was her cue to send them to the Tech Department. "Not really."

"There's a reason for it. Lawson Industries handles several software products. Some are simple bookkeeping. Others are more for 3-D designing, but the one that causes all the calls is Glamorize. It's a photo morphing program that is supposed to make average-looking people into movie stars."

The name of that software rang a bell. Even her mother talked about using it for dating pics. She said it would be easier to slim down in photos as opposed to losing weight. "I hear people are using similar software or possibly Glamorize to make dating apps pics."

"A big market. Others use it for social media posts. You've probably seen them where someone posts a photo about how they wake up looking gorgeous. Sure, they must sleep in full makeup and must never move to keep their hair perfect. The Glamorize software smooths out the skin and make wrinkles less noticeable. It can change skin tone, eye color, and even the clothes someone is wearing. These are all subtle touches. Cropping can change an image for the better, too."

"That all sounds good. So, what's the issue?"

Jaime pulled out her phone and typed into her search bar. "Okay, here's the commercial."

Della accepted the offered phone and pushed the start arrow on the video. Sad music played as a plain, overweight woman peered into a mirror. A voice-over offered to let your inner beauty be seen. The woman is later seen opening a Glamorize box. The music becomes perkier and the color more vivid as the woman uploads her photo and uses Glamorize. The image grew thinner, more beautiful, tanner, and happier. The music picked up even more as a woman who resembles the image jumped out of the picture and into a convertible with a handsome man.

"Ah, the commercial basically says change a photo, change your life."

"Oh yeah. Not only do you *not* get the happily-ever-after, but some attempts to erase extreme age or weight also end up looking strange, to say the least. There was even a lawsuit because the claims were misleading, but it was thrown out as a frivolous. Not sure why people take the ads so seriously. When I was a kid, there was an ad about troll dolls you wished on. You rubbed the doll's tummy and made a wish. In one scene, I think the girl got a unicorn. Most everyone realizes you can't get a unicorn, but not so with kids. In some ways, our complainers are disappointed children in adult bodies. They want that happily-ever-after in the commercial."

No wonder people were seething when they called. As opposed to having just faulty software, they'd been deprived of a dream. Furthermore, plenty of commercials dealt in wishful thinking with thin, fit models swilling beer and eating fast food, giving the illusion that if you bought the advertised product, you'd look like them. "I'll try to be nicer to the callers."

"Oh, you're nicer than most." She inhaled deeply, then turned back to her desk. "Back to work."

In order to look like she didn't bop over to chat, Della continued to the bathroom where she texted her mother.

Did you buy the Glamorize software?

Don't waste your money. It isn't like the commercial at all.

Some days she felt like the mother-daughter relationship was reversed. Her job would be to point out that Mabel wouldn't want someone who judged her only on appearance. Her mother would pout, raise some objections, but finally agree in the end.

I won't. Didn't Ethan stay and talk to you? Her mother could get people to open up to her. She exuded a safe, friendly, and non-judgmental manner that would have served her well as a bartender.

Nothing. He left after talking to Kyle. Della crinkled her nose. What did those two have to talk about? Her world just kept getting stranger by the day.

Any clues as to what?

You.

"Ha!" She said the word aloud instead of typing it. A flush sounded, followed by a stall opening. A woman Della didn't know walked out, cutting her eyes in her direction as she proceeded to the sink.

"I was reading a joke on my phone."

Instead of replying, she dried her hands and left the restroom, possibly thinking why someone would lurk in the restroom to read cell phone jokes. At least it was more believable than her mother's text. There had to be a reasonable answer for odd behavior and usually, it was too much liquor, which wouldn't apply at the bakery.

Her phone chimed just as she was about to drop it back into her purse. The text went by so quickly she almost missed it, but she got the gist of it.

Cannot provide chicken wings at this time. Rest of order is ready for pickup.

"What next!" She knew she should have stayed with her regular supplier. Now she'd have to go back to her standard guy for the chicken wings who'd be suspicious over why that was all she was getting. A toilet flushed and another woman exited. Not willing to manufacture another excuse, she stared at her phone, waiting for the woman to leave without talking.

A familiar voice said, "You don't have to hang out in the bathroom to use your phone. You can text while you're answering calls." Tyesha wiggled her nose. "Now, I'm not talking all the time. I realize family matters, ordering dinner and that kind of stuff would require a personal call or two. No game playing. You've got a fair boss in me, but there are others on the floor that aren't as kind. Personally, I'd like to keep you at least until all the commotion over Glamorize dies down. Before that product came out, we were good with three people. Hurry up now! People are waiting on the phones."

"Be there in a minute."

As she washed her hands, she contemplated Lawson's disappearance. It sounded like Glamorize brought in a great deal of money, but there were several photo editing programs on the market, along with photo apps on phones. Della didn't like that theory as a motivation, taking her back to the notion that Lawson left on his own which meant she had to track him down and convince him the wedding would be for the best.

The mirror reflected her grimacing face. Would that make her accessory to an unhappy marriage? People married for different reasons. Sure, she couldn't tolerate Ellie, but many men would endure her insults to have a trophy wife on their arm. Why should she get in the way of trophy wifedom?

With any luck, at lunch she'd figure out what type of car Jeffrey Lawson drove. As a big CEO, plus an eligible bachelor, he probably drove a sports car, such as a Ferrari or a Lamborghini, in an eye-catching color which would make it easy to spot. Never mind she'd never seen or even heard about an expensive car roaming the streets of Owens. It had to be something eye-catching such as a vintage Jaguar or some other type of car rich people drove. Once she knew, it could be the turning point. What if Jeffrey Lawson was really in trouble? Her hand covered her heart. She hoped not. Ethan might know, maybe. He probably knew stuff she didn't. Then again, Della might have a few tidbits that would help Ethan. What if the two of them worked together? The mirror-Della approved of the possibility, which was good enough for her.

CHAPTER NINE

O NE RAINDROP, THEN a second one splattered the windshield. Della debated about turning on the wipers—not enough rain to merit it and would probably just smear the already dirty glass. Not everything was in the same place in her mother's car or worked the same. Sure, she imagined the wipers would be on the right side of the steering column and they'd wipe away the rain if it should increase. Right now, it wasn't worth the trouble finding or using them. The infrequent patter burst into a downpour, making wipers into a necessity.

She had barely located the necessary switches before the stoplight changed to green, starting a slow chain reaction in the cars ahead of her. So far, as she turned past the hospital, there were no issues.

Recently, the hospital had started putting the names of children born there on their digital sign. Due to Owens's meager population boom, some of the names were weeks old and others, months old. The sign glowed with Sunshine's name and birth date. Della blew out a breath, wondering how such a name would impact the girl in the future. It had to be better than Della Delacroix. Fewer raindrops had her dialing back the speed on the wipers. If only to lower the intensity of the loud swish, swish, squeak refrain.

The memory of their luncheon discussion set up residence in her thoughts. Her goal for the day had focused on getting her co-workers to reveal Lawson's car of choice. It could be the man had more than one vehicle. Even though Ellie and Jeffrey had visited her bakery to discuss catering options on more than one occasion, she never took note of the car they drove. Ellie only complained about the ride.

Della's lips twisted as she tried to remember but failed to come up with more before they broke for lunch.

Tyesha, while not exactly an avalanche of information, had pointed to the cracked vinyl on the conference chairs and said, "Don't expect anything new soon. Young Lawson isn't a bit like his father, who cared about appearances." She grimaced before adding, "Come to think of it, old Lawson didn't care about the interior of the Customer Advantage area because no one comes here. He did insist that the lobby and his office were freshened up every year or so. I doubt they'll ever be freshened again. Young Lawson drives one of those foreign compact cars the color of dirt. If the man won't spring for something nice for himself, we'll get nada."

A TAN, COMPACT car lingered at the hospital exit, waiting to turn. It was nothing to catch the eye as cars go. It was an ordinary sedan without even a pleasing color to recommend it. Still, something about it nagged to be remembered. The brief image of the vehicle and its driver and passenger was conveniently filed and stored in her brain as she maneuvered the back streets, trying to save time.

Going to two stores to pick up supplies gobbled up her time which should be used for making the goodies for the speed dating event. She'd be up all night. Della had tried to talk her way around showing up tomorrow, but Tyesha pleaded with her to work the morning shift and take off at lunch. Temps could quit and not bother to mention they were going to. Other people might do that, but Della believed in treating others with respect. Besides, every extra dollar helped.

She glanced at her rearview mirror, surprised to see the same sedan she'd passed at the hospital behind her. The ashen-faced man gripped the wheel while the red-headed woman next to him chatted with her phone up to her ear. Odd. Something about the man rang a bell. Sure, there were plenty of stressed-out drivers motoring about with the slow traffic. *Wait.* Old foreign compact car? The color of dirt? Plus, a man who resembled her missing groom?

No, it couldn't be. Plenty of people had mentioned over the years how she resembled their cousin, co-worker, neighbor, or friend. She could serve as a template for your average, white, plump chick with brown hair. Maybe the same could be said of Jeffrey, except the chick and plump part.

The side street boasted only two lanes. Della slowed, hoping to get a better look at the driver. At the same time, the clouds opened and dumped gallons of water on her. She could have been underneath the giant bucket at the amusement park. The unexpected deluge forced her to turn on the lights, and defroster, as she drove. When she glanced into her rearview mirror, the heavy rain made everything a shimmery grey. There was no car to be seen or headlights penetrating the rain.

She slapped her hand on the steering wheel. What were the possibilities that the missing bridegroom had popped up behind her? Not likely. If he had, what was with the redheaded woman? As hard as she tried, Della couldn't bring back the image in the rearview mirror—a flash at the most and not surprisingly, she saw Jeffrey

Lawson everywhere or at least, men with similar features.

The wipers squeaked as the rain lessened. Della took the opportunity to check out her mirror once more. There were no vehicles behind her, which struck her as unusual. Maybe she just imagined it all. Della drove as her mind did mental gymnastics to create scenarios for her missing bridegroom. Maybe the woman had a gun on the driver, his pale face and hard grip signaling something being wrong. Then again, the couple could be married, and the woman just mentioned her mother's upcoming long visit.

So far, she had no great clues and no ransom that she knew about. She couldn't be sure, but she suspected the police were clueless. As far as that was concerned, had anyone even filed a missing person report? Her mother traded in gossip and had her finger in every pie. Come to think of it, didn't she have a friend who was a police dispatcher? As a teen, she used to refer to the woman as Cackling Chain Smoker. Della hadn't been a fan, but her mother explained the association by saying they'd been friends since grade school. The implication being you just didn't drop people who you'd known forever.

A few minutes later, she found herself entering a traffic circle. Her thoughts were on which exit to take to reach the unfamiliar store when the tan sedan popped up again. Her eyes bugged as she veered into the second exit to follow the car. This time they weren't getting away. Her fingers tightened as she firmed her jaw, determined to follow. The only problem was what would she do once they stopped. Would she jump out of the car and shout, "Catering Emergency?"

Technically, if Lawson had left of his own volition, his behavior might be out of character, but as an adult, he could do what he wanted. What if he was being coerced, possibly brainwashed into giving up company secrets, or even kidnapped? Not knowing what to do when her target stopped, she felt for her phone. Locating her cell, she managed to call her mother. The ringing phone came over the speakers.

Her mother answered. "Hey, sweetie. What's up?"

"Problems. I may be following our bridegroom and an unknown female. I'm not sure what to do. My expectation included a thoughtful conversation, not a car chase and an unexpected stranger."

"You're not speeding?" Concern, evident in Mabel's voice, carried over the airwaves.

"No." She rolled her eyes. *Typical.* One speeding ticket when she was seventeen branded her as a wannabe drag racer. "Following, but not being obvious about it. No worries about your car."

A sigh carried over the line. "Not so much about the car. I just don't want you to attract attention. I may have forgotten to put the sticker tag on the license plate. It's in the car with the registration. Whenever you stop, you might want to slap it on. I can't afford a ticket." She whistled. "They're none too cheap."

"Will do," Della agreed and wondered just how much an expired tags fine was. She had no clue, but apparently, her mother did.

The suspect sedan slowed, flipped on the blinker, and made a slow turn into the parking lot of a vet's office. She had no choice but to follow, but not having a pet could be an issue. Her teeth clamped together as she faced the fact that she had no real plan. Sure, she hoped to have a logical talk with the man, explaining that he couldn't just run away. Maybe she should ask him if he needed help. It would be hard to do either with the woman beside him.

Della chose a spot a few spaces away, parked, and then pretended to look at her phone, wondering what Ethan Stone would do in such a situation. Besides looking the part of a private investigator, he wouldn't be stupid enough to be seen. Outside of that, she had no clue what Ethan would do.

The redhead popped out of the car while the man Della thought was Lawson followed more slowly. He opened the back door and assisted a small mop-like dog out and clicked on a sparkly leash.

The three of them strolled toward the office doors where the dog balked and refused to go any farther. The man she assumed to be Jeffrey Lawson squatted and swept the dog up into his arms. Not exactly the behavior of a man being coerced or held for ransom. Perhaps her eyes on him caused him to turn and glare at her. At that moment, Della noticed the soul patch under his bottom lip. Not her guy. Clean-shaven Jeffrey Lawson would never sport a stubble patch that indicated poor shaving skills or an attempt to be a hipster. Maybe it was a musician thing since she saw more guys in start-up bands sporting beards with such meticulous lines that it must take forever to get ready.

Her eyelids fluttered closed as she exhaled. There was no big confrontation, which worked since she normally avoided conflict. Why did Lawson have to look like half of the mid-thirty male population of Owens? Della blew out a sigh. The man's insistence on driving an aging compact that had seen better days was no help, either.

Della checked her dash clock and grunted. Her little detour had cost her precious time. Most of the suppliers who sold to restaurants and caterers tended to close by six, but if she got in the door, they'd have to wait on her. Since this would call for a little more speed than normal, she better slap the sticker on the plate.

CHAPTER TEN

DELLA USED HER hip to keep the bakery back door open since boxes weighed down her arms. "Mom, I'm back!"

The familiar sound of her mother talking carried into the kitchen. Oops. Maybe she shouldn't have assumed no one was in the front of the store. It was not professional of her, shouting as soon as she entered. Her gaze focused on the swinging door that separated the two areas.

"Oh no," her mother said to someone on the other side of the door. "That's not what I said. I think the mixer will be perfect for you. Why don't you come?"

"Good grief." Della slammed the frozen food on the stainless-steel countertop. Her mother had already invited Ethan to the speed dating event. There was no telling how he took the invitation. Perhaps he regarded her mother as a modern woman who went after what she wanted. In that regard, she was, but her interest in Ethan leaned toward a potential date for her daughter, not herself.

Nothing says needy like your mother trying to score a date for you. She'd have to put a stop to that. Her hands went up to her hair, trying to fluff what had to be flat hair at this time of night. A downward tug on her shirt smoothed that out some. It was probably the best she could achieve. Inhaling deeply, she placed her hand on the door, stalling for a moment, trying to decide how to defuse the situation. All she really had to do was interrupt the conversation—tell a funny story, change the subject, or ask Ethan about his day.

Her mind made up, Della pushed her lips up into her practiced work smile. "Hello."

The total lack of people in the shop area, especially Ethan Stone, struck her first. Her mother leaned against the counter, tilting slightly toward the front of the store as she continued to talk on her cell. She wiggled her free hand when she spotted Della. One index finger went up indicating only a minute more.

"Just consider it. It's not exactly like men are knocking on your door. Okay. See ya."

At least she didn't have to consider what to say to Ethan—one less thing to worry about. Della waited until her mother pocketed the phone.

"Cindy." Mabel gave a little nod and continued. "Her husband died last year. The woman isn't opposed to remarrying, but she never goes anywhere to meet anyone. I'm trying to encourage her."

Never mind that her mother could have been describing herself instead of Cindy. As far as encouragement, Della had tried. Her mother shone when taking care of others. Currently, Della served as her pet project, but hopefully, that wouldn't be forever. Even though her independent mother often would try things her similar-aged friends wouldn't, Mabel drew the line at solo dining, movies, or travel—all things she loved.

"That's nice. You should tell her you're going."

Her mother sniffed. "Not sure if I can."

Did she hear her right? Wasn't this the woman who signed up both of them? Della's eyebrows arched as she crossed her arms. "Excuse me? I know you signed us both up. We'll be there. You even talked Clarice into helping with the buffet table so we could mingle. Now you're ducking out on me?"

"Not exactly," Mabel spoke as she picked up a cloth, wiping down already clean surfaces. "It seems silly."

Desperate. Crazy. Those were the words that came to Della, but her mother had acted excited about it, even if she was only hopeful for her daughter. "I don't know. It's how you look at it." She scratched her head, trying to come up with a way to encourage her mother. Suddenly, she took on her mother's role. "I read about this guy who was so terrified to date he threw up at the thought. He hired a dating coach who put him through six of these speed dating things. The coach told him he didn't have to date any of the women he met. That took off the pressure. All he had to do was be pleasant, have fun, and ask some of the women for their numbers or business cards."

Her mother stopped wiping and turned to listen. "What happened to the fellow?"

"He did end up going out with some of the women he met. One of them had a friend who she thought he'd be perfect for and introduced them. They've been together ever since. There you go." She turned to grab a drink so as not to face her mother, who could spot a lie at ten feet. The last part she improvised since the article hadn't followed up on the guy. It *could* have happened.

Her mother tapped her temple. "I remember that story. I think he was on *Millionaire Matchmaker*." She grinned, moved close to Della, and patted her cheek. "You always know what to say."

"I learned it from you."

"There you go again." Mabel chuckled. "Let's get started on the food, so we can squeeze in a few hours of beauty sleep. Whatever happened with the car you were following?"

"I don't want to talk about it." She nudged her mother as they moved into the kitchen. "The good news is your sticker is on your license plate."

Mabel nudged her back. "Wonderful. Horace came by and checked your car. It's just a radiator leak."

Dollar signs flashed in front of her eyes, causing her to groan. "How much?"

"Well…" Her mother stretched out the word. "Horace told me most mechanics will charge about a hundred dollars or more. For an experienced mechanic, it takes about fifteen dollars of supplies and ten minutes of work."

It sounded like a build-up. Maybe Horace would do it for only ninety-nine dollars. Exhaustion weighed on her, and this one more thing felt like an oversized buzzard landing on her shoulder. "How much?"

"A cup of coffee."

"What did you say?"

"Coffee. He's willing to work for coffee. At first, he offered to do it free since you are family and all our cars always went to his shop. We've probably spent hundreds, maybe thousands over the past three decades. I told him you wouldn't feel right accepting some-thing for free."

Della cut her eyes to her mother. Not accept *free*? Did this wom-an even know her? "So, when is he going to work on the car?"

"He already did. You can drive it home tonight. If you meet someone special and want to spend more time talking, I can load up and drive back to the bakery."

"Dream on." If only her mother had the same optimism about

herself.

THE BAR BOASTED a tiny kitchen featuring a griddle, fridge, and three fry baskets waiting over oil that smelled none too fresh. Della stacked the covered pans on the counter and turned to take another pan from her mother. They'd perfected the bucket pass method of unloading from their previous events. It depended on being able to park close, which worked this time.

Clarice bustled into the kitchen. "There you are!" She placed both hands on her ample hips and shot them a scolding look. "I was beginning to get worried."

Rather than reply, Della left it to her mother to calm down her overly made-up friend. She had setting up down to an art form. The event didn't technically start for thirty minutes. First, she organized the pans in the order she wanted them to go out, but it took a great deal of weaving around Clarice to do so.

"Mom, could you and Clarice go set up the table?"

Understanding the situation, Mabel grabbed the box with the linens, pan stands, sterno cans, lighter, and most importantly, business cards to set out. The food she warmed before was packed into heat keeping bags, like what pizza delivery used. Thank goodness she brought along her air fryer to reheat the French-fried green beans in case they needed it. There was no way she'd use whatever was in the fry vats. She had standards.

The low burble of conversation meant a jump on the mingling, which Della assumed was all good, although how much could you find out in seven minutes? She hefted big pans of macaroni and cheese bites and backed out of the door at the same time as an ear-splitting buzz ripped through the air. Della froze, gripping the pan for dear life.

Clarice yelled, "Too loud! Too harsh! Don't you have something like a tinkling bell?"

Oh, that's all it was. She swung around in search of the table her mother had prepared. The red tablecloth she used, embossed with hearts for Cupid's Catering Company, worked perfectly for the event. It hid marinara stains, too. Mabel stood by the table, already chatting with a man. Looked like a win for Mom. She guided the pan into the frame and lit the sterno can. Curious, she leaned the tiniest bit forward to peek at the man who had caught her mother's interest. The man turned, gave a slight nod, and gave her a rakish grin that would make him very popular. *Ethan Stone*. He came after all.

"Oh, hi." Realizing she'd been caught gawking, Della reached for an excuse. "I was checking to see how many people are here. Gotta make sure we brought enough food." Gosh, she hoped no one else heard that. It didn't make her sound like a competent caterer. "Better go get the rest of the food."

Ethan patted his flat stomach. "After eating so many of your delicious cookies, I can't wait to see what you brought."

Participants with drinks in hand cast glances in the direction of the buffet table. Della smiled and then turned to retrieve more pans. It would help if someone would assist her, but her mother kept the crowd at bay while Clarice searched for a tinkling bell. All things considered, if sixty or more people were talking at once, the buzzer might be more practical.

Six more trips and everything was out on the table. Della moved the napkins at an angle to the plates, making it more artistic. Aware of the growing crowd surging ever closer, she removed the foil tops and enjoyed the swell of excited voices. Maybe the participants might not make a romantic connection, but a few might fall hopelessly in love with her food. She should say something.

"Tonight's buffet is brought to you by Cupid's Catering Company, located on Bank Square, serving your catering, snack, and bakery needs. Enjoy!"

She barely got the last word out before hands reached for plates. Donning a plastic serving glove, she caught her mother's eye and she joined her behind the buffet line. The bigger question—where was Clarice? Brownies and fruit kebobs were on individual plates which allowed people to pick them up and go. After an initial rush of about thirty people, the line slowed down, allowing Della to evaluate what trays needed to be exchanged. The wings went fast, as expected, as did the macaroni.

Some static sounded, and then Clarice said, "Testing, one, two, three! Can you hear me?"

A few people shouted *yes*, but apparently not enough because she said even louder, "I can't hear you!"

A chorus of people not only yelled but waved, too. Clarice launched into a long-winded analogy about love being a precious gift while Mabel made a slashing motion to cut it short. When that didn't work, she circled her hand to wind it up. Finally, Clarice said, "You have five minutes per table. When you hear this sound..." She pointed to the man standing by a karaoke machine which emitted a blast that sounded like someone blowing a raspberry into the air. "... the women will move on to the next man. Since only forty-seven participants showed up, this should only take about two hours."

Della leaned toward her mother. "I thought they had seven

minutes."

"Someone forgot to do the math. They closed the bar for the event, but they have a popular live band later. Patrons pay a cover charge. I hear it's well attended, which means they need to get the hopeful daters out."

"We'll need to clear out, too. I don't want the band fans to think they missed out on the eats and be upset about it."

Her mother bobbed her head in agreement and pointed to one of the serving pans. "Looks like the green beans are going."

It was sooner than she expected, and she didn't have any in the air fryer, reheating. While people like classic bar food, it wasn't much good cold. "Watch the table for me."

The loud raspberry indicated the dating had started. Della exited the bar thinking why in the world had anyone thought that sound served in the game of romance. It reminded her of primary students blowing raspberries at each other, which usually meant disgust, ridicule, and basically nothing good. The participants who probably talked themselves into coming—if they didn't have a parent who signed them up—were probably ready to leave at hearing it.

Inside the minuscule bar kitchen, she toasted the green beans, thankful she'd decided to bring the air fryer along at the last minute. High-pitched, shrill laughter wormed its way into the tiny, hot room. Well, at least she wasn't out there laughing like a hyena at some guy's bad joke. Rather than a response to a witticism, laughter often came from nerves.

Participating would be the equivalent of a root canal without anesthesia or a never-ending job interview with twenty different guys. No thanks. A bead of sweat rolled down her face, leaving a track in the foundation she'd donned at her mother's insistence. Her mother's old school beliefs included squeezing into shapewear, full makeup, and even wigs or hair extensions to create an illusion. Never mind the real person didn't look like that. Not Della, though. A person would have to accept her as she was. If they did, she might fancy herself up for a later event.

The ticking of the air fryer timer dominated the kitchen sanctuary. Forced laughter along with the bleating of the buzzer slid around the door. Della grimaced and shook the air fryer pan, and then poured the contents onto a clean tray. She backed out of the kitchen and into a wall of sound. The aroma of barbecued wings and the heavier, indulgent note of chocolate mingled with the combined scents of hairspray, perfume, and fear. While she couldn't describe what fear smelled like, she still recognized it.

Clarice temporarily abandoned her duties as emcee to visit the buffet table. "Good job, ladies. I thought you would be participating."

"Work," Della explained, gesturing to the table, and put a thumb back to herself. "Also, I'm actually dressed for catering."

Early on she had decided on the black pants since almost every caterer wore black bottoms, but she decided against a white shirt because it only invites stains. Instead, she had black T-shirts made with the Cupid's Catering logo in silver right above the left breast. Almost nothing showed on it except for white frosting and cream sauce. Usually, the matching apron caught any wayward food stains. In that case, she removed the apron.

"No problem." Clarice bobbed her head frantically, rather like one of those desk ornaments that keeps rocking after the initial push. "I need you to participate."

"There's plenty of women out there. I saw them."

"That's the problem," Clarice said with a sniff.

"Not sure how I can help."

Clarice angled her head in the direction of a table where Ethan stood with his arms crossed as opposed to sitting. "Mr. Handsome slash Difficult refused to talk to any of the women unless he talks to you first."

"Me?" Della placed a hand on her chest as if confused about who Clarice meant. "Ethan can see me anytime in the bakery."

"All the same, he wants to talk to you now. Go talk to him, and then you can go back to moving your pans around."

Moving her pans around? Was that all she thought caterers did?

Mabel cleared her throat. "Just do it. Five minutes is a very short time. What could it hurt?"

"Please!" Clarice pushed her palms together in a prayer-like pose. "I've already had ten women hint if they didn't get time with Mr. Difficult, they wanted their money back. As you probably guess, I need the money to be able to pay you."

"Okay, okay." She handed a clean glove and a serving spoon to Clarice. "You can take my place, especially since you volunteered to help."

The gaping mouth signaled the woman couldn't remember her declaration to help. It made Della wonder about the conversation between her mother and her friend. Had Clarice been making grandiose promises to sway Mabel her way? It must have worked since they paid to be participants, and the only words Della had thus far uttered to any eligible male was "enjoy your meal."

Della took off her apron and removed the plastic serving gloves that made her hands sweat. She stopped off at the bar, grabbed an iced tea, and worked her way over to Ethan's table. A few women noticed her direction and glared. If looks could kill, she'd be bleeding to death from the stabbing stares.

"Well, hello." Della greeted Ethan and took a seat.

Ethan joined her. "Hello to you, too."

His usual calm and collected manner was still in evidence. He didn't act like a smitten man. There was no reason for him to be. The only claim she might have on him was the man could be falling for her coffee.

"What can I do for you? Rumor is you won't chat with any of the female participants until you've talked to me."

He glanced down at the table and then up at her with a smirk. "True enough. Worse, I must pay for the privilege. You're a hard woman to pin down, let alone have a decent conversation with."

She put out her hands palms up, trying to be as matter of fact as Ethan. "I'm here now."

"So, you are. We need to talk."

That much she assumed. Della kept her mouth shut and her lips firm, refusing to simper. She had no reason to believe the man would swear undying affection for her.

Ethan tapped the table with his index finger. "You've inserted yourself into a dangerous game. I'm here to warn you off."

Just as she suspected, no declarations of undying love. "How so?"

CHAPTER ELEVEN

CONVERSATIONS SWIRLED AROUND the tiny tables suitable only for two cocktail glasses and a shared appetizer. Della tried to gauge if Ethan's statement about her being in danger smacked of teasing. Even in the marginal lighting, his serious gaze and firm chin hinted more at danger than humor.

Someone must have thought the place needed some background music. A song started playing. A small part of Della's mind tried to identify the song while the rest of her wrestled with the possibility of peril. "Why am I in danger? I bet it's not my delicious coffee."

"No. You would have been safer if you'd stayed in your bakery."

There's nothing like a cryptic conversation to make things even more confusing. She inhaled deeply, ready to dig more into a conversation heading nowhere. Her mom adored Ethan, but that didn't mean the guy wasn't missing a few screws. Her hand covered her face, and she groaned. "Oh no. I can't believe it."

"What?" Ethan raised a little in his seat and leaned over the table. There was concern evident in his expression.

"They're playing that song about the woman who vandalized the guy's car because he's a cheater. Not exactly what you want at a speed dating event. Most women are aware men cheat. There's no reason to broadcast the reminder during a dating event. Better a woman should have the delightful first quarter of the romance where she adores the guy. By the third quarter, she'll realize on her own what a true rat fink he is. I mean, if you go in with that third quarter attitude, why even bother dating? It would save a lot of trouble and heartache."

Ethan retook his seat, mumbled indecipherably, and reached out to cover Della's hand with his own. "Sounds to me like you've had some experience in the matter."

"Mother." She growled the word. If Della had siblings, there would be someone else for her parent to natter on about to strangers.

Ethan rubbed his thumb over the back of her hand before removing it. "Don't go getting angry with Mabel. She didn't say anything. Told me you were single, but that was it."

The music stopped long enough for the infamous raspberry. Della stood up, ready to return to the buffet station. Ethan snagged her hand. "You can't go. We didn't talk about how you're in danger."

"That might be important." If he wasn't acting so sincere, she'd normally blow it off. Della lingered, not sure what to do. Her nose twitched as the scent of burnt barbecue sauce teased it. She should be moving the wings around in the pan and spooning sauce over them. The fact any wings remained showed how serious the participants were, or perhaps they were afraid of smearing sauce on their clothes and being labeled a slob.

A redhead in skyscraper heels and a top cut low enough to stop traffic shoved Della aside saying, "You've had him to yourself long enough. We all deserve a go."

Not wanting to engage in a confrontation, Della turned and walked back to the buffet table where her mother chatted with a middle-aged, balding man. At her arrival, the man drifted away, saying something about getting back to work.

"Well, well," Della teased as she inserted her hand into a serving glove. "Looks like you don't even need to do the table rounds since the men come to you."

"Nope." She snorted and shook her head. "That's Oscar. He owns the place and bartends on the weekends when it gets busy."

"Uh huh." Della picked up the spoon and rearranged the wings. "Wherever you go, you attract men of a certain age."

Her mother laughed. "It could be they feel safe around me. I'm not their ex or their mother-in-law, and I'm not on the prowl for a new husband. Besides, I'm at the right age to know the lyrics from all the Beatles and Everly Brothers songs. Plus, I know Eartha Kitt sang the original "Santa Baby." Usually, I share a mutual respect with men my age for Joe Namath, but possibly for different reasons. Add to that I used to own a 1965 Mustang—not in 65, though. This makes me a dream conversationalist."

"Wow!" She waggled her eyebrows. "No wonder you attract the men. With whom else could they discuss their mutual love for cars and football?"

"Laugh if you want." Mabel waved away her daughter's faked astonishment. "What I want to know is what Ethan was so hot to talk to you about."

That was a good question and one she didn't know the answer to. "Mom. You're a pretty good judge of people. Do you think Ethan is on the level?"

Her mother pursed her lips, and then glanced back at the man in question, causing Della to do likewise. The normally cool and collected Ethan leaned away from the redhead who resembled a lioness who'd spotted her dinner by the way she crouched over the table, waiting for the optimal moment to pounce. Their combined stares must have caught his eye because he formed his thumb and pinkie into a phone gesture and held it to his ear.

"It looks like he wants us to call," Della observed. "I don't have his number."

Mabel patted down her pants pockets and pulled out her cell. "I have it. Lucky for him, I put it in my phone." She held her phone up and moved into better light before scrolling and tapping the number.

Ethan jumped up, pulled out his phone, and said something that had the redhead crossing her arms and sulking. His long strides carried him to the buffet table as he spoke into the phone. "Thank you! I owe you. Can you find me someplace to hide from Ms. Hungry and Desperate?"

The kitchen served as a good bet since there'd be no reason for anyone to go inside. Without saying a word, keeping her hand low at her hip, she made a subtle follow-me gesture, picked up the pan of wings, and headed for the kitchen. Inside the kitchen, she placed the pan down and searched for her replacement pan. The door swung open, revealing Ethan with the phone still glued to his ear.

He heaved a sigh and pocketed his phone. "As an investigator, I've been in some tight spots, but none that came out of nowhere. Starr came at me like a meteorite burning through the atmosphere. *Meteor* might have been a more apt name for her."

Men complained about women chasing them, but they must secretly enjoy it. "Oh, you poor thing. Was she wolf-whistling you? Undressing you with her eyes?"

"No. She told me she needed to get married within a month to beat her ex to the altar and offered me five thousand dollars to do so." His hand went up to rub his neck. "She wasn't taking no for an answer. What's up with this town?"

"I'm sure we have the same number of crazies as the next burg. It's your fault for being so irresistible."

"Oh…" Ethan purred the word and leaned against the counter with a smirk. "You hid your feelings well."

Typical. He twisted her words around to suit himself. Della inserted a slotted serving spoon into the chicken wings, stirring a little more vigorously than necessary. One wing flew out and skidded across the floor, leaving a red barbecued trail.

"Fudge!" She ripped off the paper towel from the roll mounted on the wall. From her position on the floor, Della addressed the mistaken assumption. "I didn't say I found you delectable. Starshine, or whatever her name was, wanted you as her mister. I can do without any more remarks like that. No need to make this kitchen look like a crime scene."

A more somber mien replaced Ethan's amused expression. He inhaled deeply. "That's what I need to talk to you about."

That sounded serious. Della balled the paper towel and slowly rose to her feet. "Go ahead. I've got to admit I'm curious about the danger. Am I underpricing my bakery goods? I think so, too." She shrugged. "No one really knows me yet, and I need a competitive edge. Cheap tends to get noticed."

"So do people snooping around Jeffrey Lawson. I imagine you've already attracted attention." Ethan scratched his jaw and lifted one eyebrow. "Somehow you wrangled the security guard into your plan."

"How do you know he's not my boyfriend?" Della smoothed the

foil top over the wings for their trip to the buffet. There was no reason to take any chances of food flying across the room. Even though she feigned disinterest, she tensed as she awaited Ethan's response.

"He's not your type."

"You know my type?"

"Not really, but the two of you were awkward, like two ill-fitting puzzle pieces trying to connect, but not succeeding." He worked his chin to one side, and then the other, as if pondering the possibility.

As much as Della hated to admit it, Ethan had summed up her non-relationship with Kyle. "Okay, he's not the love of my life, but I'm single. I can see people." She threw up her hands. "I'm *here* for Pete's sake."

"True," he agreed. "Only as a caterer not as a participant. You were conned into registering by Clarice."

"You know this how?" Before he could answer, Della did. "My mother."

"I wouldn't consider it top secret information. Besides, they listed the names of the participants, which I find very unethical. My employer wouldn't be pleased to see my name on some speed dating form when I'm being paid to find Lawson."

Della's mouth dropped open, and her eyes popped. "I'm on some paper!" She pressed a hand against her chest. "The horrors. The very idea makes me feel like a 4-H cow up for auction. I need to talk to Mother and Clarice."

"Wait!" Ethan grasped her arm. "You can rant at later. I need you to listen to me now. Trust me when I say you could be in danger."

"You keep saying that. I assume you were hired by the family to keep things hush-hush."

"I imagine the family would like to keep things quiet since the truth could hurt the company. As I told you, I'm an investigator and work for different folks for various purposes. Right now, Lawson Industries is being slapped with a copyright infringement suit. Apparently, Glamorize is not their product, but was lifted from an overseas software design company. They went through the usual cease and desist request to no effect. My job is basically to find him and serve papers. No luck so far, but the original creator or possibly his company has sent out enforcers."

"Um, like in the movies. Beefy dudes who dress in black with bad attitudes and tire irons."

"I don't know about the clothing choices, but I imagine they're packing more than tire irons." He gave her arm a gentle squeeze before releasing it. "This is why I'm warning you off. Basically, I got a call to be careful. I can't identify these people. They only want to get to Lawson. If they think you know anything, they might grab you and force you to tell."

"I don't know anything."

"They don't know that."

Her teeth worried her bottom lip as the hair on the back of her neck lifted. This was bad—not radiator leak bad, but movie of the week bad. With any luck, she missed catching the attention of any hired thugs. Owens could do without the criminal element, as could her bakery. "What can I do? I certainly don't need any wannabe hitmen hanging out at the bakery and ordering espressos."

"Ditto that." He tapped two fingers against his chest. "I need to find Lawson and explain the situation. Get him to deal with reality as opposed to hiding from it."

All this time she assumed Lawson's absence indicated cold feet as far as the wedding. What if he hid to protect Ellie? That meant the wedding could still happen. Her muscles relaxed from their former clenched position. She sighed and then rocked forward on her toes, doing her best to be eye to eye with Ethan. "You have to find Jeffrey Lawson."

"That's what I'm doing." He shot her a quizzical look from under beetled eyebrows.

"Try harder." She pushed the words out through clenched teeth. "My catering career depends on this."

"All right. Personally, I'd think you'd be a little bit more worried about your wellbeing. We need to share information. You might have information that would lead to Lawson."

Della dropped down on her heels and exhaled. Sharing information made sense, but something told her it would be a one-way street as far as sharing. What if Ethan, if that was his real name, was the actual thug? It sounded like something a clever enforcer might say. The best she could do was stall for time. "I need to get these wings out."

CHAPTER TWELVE

THE DAY AFTER a catered event ranked as Della's least favorite thing in her chosen career—the multitude of dirty pans. Normally, she tried to do the dishes when she came back but not last night. The speed dating went over its allotted time. Most participants hadn't made a love connection but were content to stand around, pick the buffet bare, and listen to the cover band that served as the live music. Oscar, the owner, split his time between chatting with Mabel, band members, and the bouncer. In the end, he must have decided he'd not get any more money out of the speed daters for a cover charge since they hadn't left before the music started. His best bet would be they'd drink more.

Della turned on the water in the bakery's oversized sink. Finding the defunct Hillbilly Fixin's restaurant space been a miracle. Before signing the lease, she'd never been inside the shop as a customer. Like most of Owens's populace, she'd been suspect of the possible ingredients they served due to the picturesque name. It was a good bet most of the food left the shop wrapped in foil, which explained why the previous owners didn't invest in a commercial dishwasher. It may have been something to do with the washers being outrageously expensive, too.

Several squirts of dish liquid and beating the water with her hand created a surplus of bubbles for the pans. The back door opened as soon she immersed the first greasy pan. No one except her mother had a key. "Hi, Mom! What are you doing here? Shouldn't you be sleeping in or something?"

"As if I could, knowing my only daughter would be slaving away on the weekend."

"Hey, it comes with the territory. Weekends are my busy time. People are more likely to pop in for a treat when they don't have to rush back to work."

"Makes sense." Mabel swung her oversized purse up onto the counter. "Besides, I want a recap on the speed dating event."

"You were there. Maybe I should be asking you for a recap."

"I'd say they ate like they hadn't eaten in a week. Several of the men were taken with you."

Della placed her soapy hands on her hips and regarded her mother with a disbelieving expression. "Get real. I didn't talk to anyone. Not sure how I could make an impression, good or otherwise."

"We got several compliments on the food. People naturally assume older women cook. When I pointed out that you were the chef, the men acted impressed."

She should have known. Verbal embroidery happened to be a major part of Mabel's skillset. She could take a simple remark, analyze it for meaning, and paraphrase it. It was rather like the old game often called *telephone* or *gossip* where people whispered a simple phrase to each other. The phrase at the end of a long line bore no resemblance to the original one.

"I'm sure they were happy to get food they didn't cook. It made no difference who cooked it." It was just like her mother to parlay a simple comment about food into an attraction to the cook. "Since you're here, you can start the coffee. I have a few regulars who always come by, and I'd hate to disappoint them. The oven is warming up, and I'll pop in the pastries."

"Glad to." Her mother pulled out the premixed coffee container from the fridge and headed to the front of the store where the coffee maker was. Before she passed through the door, she smirked at her daughter. "I'll want to hear all about the little tête-à-tête between you and Ethan."

Hope springs eternal in a mother's heart. Della pushed another pan into the water as the oven chimed. A flat pan of cheese danishes and another of apricot awaited their turn in the oven. The danishes won over cookies on the weekends, although she played with the idea of donuts. Owens boasted at least two donut shops which had their own following. It may be difficult to break into the donut market.

"Tell all," her mother instructed, reentering the kitchen, and pulling up a stool. "You should have seen how angry the redhead got when she saw Ethan go into the kitchen after you did."

"I'm not sure why. For all she knew, it could have been an exit. Trust me; it was not a romantic meeting. No sweet nothings were whispered. Basically, he warned me off looking for Lawson. Our clean-shaven groom isn't as upright and outstanding as we thought."

Mabel rubbed her hand over her face. "I can't believe that. He's such a nice young man, considering he puts up with the antics of his bride-to-be. It would take a saint to handle her."

Her mother had a valid point, but Ethan wouldn't be chasing after a saint. "Well, apparently Glamorize, the company's biggest seller, is a rip-off of someone else's program. It's a foreign product that a developer hoped wouldn't be recognized under a different name. I don't think this can be pinned on Lawson personally. I heard he doesn't even develop anything. His job is basically marketing or at least overseeing it."

"That's all bosses ever do, is oversee stuff. Still, I think there's an obligation to make sure your company isn't hijacking someone else's intellectual property."

Della hadn't given the whole matter a great deal of thought, except for dangerous types lurking around to see if Ethan had succeeded in his mission.

"Hmmm…"

It was hard to know what happened. Why would someone pay for a private investigator if they didn't have a case? Lawsuits filled the courthouse, alleging someone stole someone else's intellectual property, be it plot, song, play, or software. How often could people come up with the exact same idea?

Apparently, quite often, according to the news articles she read. An artist could be influenced by something they read or heard and even include parts of it in their own work without being accused of copyright infringement. Her high school English teacher had different thoughts on the same subject. In her opinion, three significant words in the same order in a sentence equaled copying. A student could type call me and be okay, but once they added Ishmael, making it the opening line of *Moby Dick*, they got a big fat zero and a call home.

She considered the possibility that Lawson didn't do a legal search on his software or was unaware that one was even done. It could be that the copyright lawyers handled those details. "Maybe they should have done some type of research first. I'm not sure what the rules are. Ethan is wanting to find him for copyright infringement, which is covered by a type of insurance. He told me whatever country or company that's involved has also sent in some unsavory types since they're tired of waiting. They're possibly also weary of Lawson raking in all the money. Nearly all the complaint calls we get are about Glamorize. It doesn't sound like a great program to me."

Her mother sighed. "All a person has to do is buy it once. There are no returns on software, no matter how bad it is. I should know."

Sometimes being an adult meant not mentioning stuff. She knew her mother had bought Glamorize for her dating profile, and it hadn't worked out the way she'd wanted. "Maybe the two of us don't know Jeffrey Lawson at all. Maybe he isn't the straight-up guy we thought he was. It could be he used his freshly scrubbed image to make dirty business deals. When the heat became too much, he vanished, leaving everyone else out to hang."

"Oh, sweetie. I hate to think badly about anyone." She shook her head slowly and slid off the stool. "Let me take over the dishes, and you can get the shop ready. After all, you're the face of the business. You should be out front."

"Okay." Della checked the cheese pastries and pulled them out. Timers worked most of the time, but nothing beat a visual inspection. She had a platter with a large doily awaiting the delicacies. Pounding sounded on the front door, followed by yelling. "Let me in!"

Della tensed with the hot pan in hand. It never occurred to her one of the heavies could be a woman or that she would take such a direct approach. She eased the pan onto the table and attempted to peek out the door, which wasn't easy with her mother trying to do likewise.

"It's Ellie, and it's not even seven. What could she want?"

"Remember what I said about not wanting to speak badly about people?" Mabel whispered the words. "For her, I'd make an exception."

The pounding started up again. "I know you're in there! It's important!"

Della already told the woman there would be no menu changes and was glad she didn't have the burden of making the wedding cake. What else could there be? "It could be she's heard from Jeffrey. We need to let her in."

Before doing so, she ran her hands over her face, checking for any flour. She donned her high chef hat, feeling it gave her authority—not that Ellie would recognize it. The constant banging continued despite Della being easily seen walking to the door. Anyone else would have stopped. Even though she hated doing it, Della lunged the last few steps to save the glass in the door.

She flung the door open to the crisp morning air. "Come in."

Her tone could have been a little more cordial, but to her merit, she *did* answer the door. Ellie blew in with the same vigor as the wind, disturbing the cozy atmosphere of the bakery and rattling the placards advertising coffee flavors and bagel selections. On second thought, the wind must have unsettled the signs, but she wasn't willing to bet on it.

"About time," Ellie huffed and crossed her arms. "I could have frozen to death outside. How'd that look? My frozen, yet still beautiful body resting against your door."

Several replies developed, including it wasn't that cold or maybe dress appropriately for the season. Fortunately, they never made their way past her lips. Instead, Della said, "But fortunately, you didn't. What has you out before store hours?"

"Store hours?" Bridezilla's brow furrowed and her lips pursed. "I'm a customer, a paying customer. There are no store hours for me."

Knowing her ability to fabricate was nil, Della covered her face briefly with her hand to hide any emotions. Then she faked a yawn. There was no need to mention the bridegroom paid the deposit and not her royal highness, who tapped the toe of her high heel boot to indicate her impatience.

"It's really early. What has you rushing here?"

"Black tiger shrimp." Ellie stretched her acrylic nail tipped fore-finger and thumb about six inches apart. "The really big ones."

Even though Della knew this was an ambush attempt to change the menu without her groom around to rein in her extravagant tendencies, she chose to play dumb. "Black tiger shrimp." She echoed the words. "They do tend to be bigger than most shrimp. However, there are different grades of black tiger shrimp, too."

"I need the biggest!" At this point, Ellie stretched both hands about a foot apart. "I want to show everyone in this one-horse town what quality is."

Della's hand went back to rub her neck and she wondered how to defuse the situation. One thing she knew was Ellie wouldn't know quality, even if it came in the form of a foot-long shrimp slapping her in the face.

"You need a foot-long shrimp? Maybe you should check out Leo's Fish and Pet Shop on Market Street. I imagine it's a unique present for the groom. At least you won't have to take it on a walk."

Maybe Della had gone too far because Ellie stomped her foot and gave a growl reminiscent of an angry Chihuahua. "What's wrong with you? Are you just another moron in the whole gaggle of idiot wedding vendors?"

It sounded like Della wasn't the only one who'd received a personal morning visit from Bridezilla. "If you're wanting to add tiger shrimp to the menu, it's a hard no. We talked about this. The supplies must be ordered. Many items are made ahead of time or at least started. It's not like I'm whipping up dinner for four. Tiger shrimp is an expensive item—"

Ellie interrupted. "That's why I want it!"

The woman didn't even let Della finish. Still, she had a point to make. "My suppliers don't keep a large stock of tiger shrimp because there isn't much call for it. Most folks make do with large or extra-large white shrimp."

Aggravation wafted off the female. "I'm not most folks. I want what I want."

Even though her business depended on the big event, she had half a mind to find Jeffrey and tell him to run for his life. Change his name. Leave everything behind. Whatever he needed to do to get away from Bridezilla. She struck her as the type who would file a breach of promise lawsuit if the wedding didn't happen.

"We discussed this. The menu is set. It's a great menu. Friends and family will be impressed, especially with your extravagant cookie bar. No one has ever had so many varieties of cookies."

Even though it was popular in the Midwest, Della had pushed the cookie bar idea to showcase her treats.

Another guttural growl erupted as Ellie fisted her hands. "That's not good enough. I'll get someone else to cater the event. It'll be your loss."

Forget trying to find the missing groom. Della saw the building block of future bookings melting away like an ice sculpture at an outdoor wedding due to a red-faced spoiled brat. She swallowed hard, trying to organize her thoughts. Her one foot slid back followed by the other to stay out of slapping range.

The kitchen door swung open and Mabel bustled out. "Good luck with that! No caterer will take you in the tri-county region. It's too late. You'll lose the deposit your groom paid. We can take you to court for not honoring your contract."

"Well, I, um…" The woman turned with a huff and marched out the door, slamming it hard enough to vibrate the glass.

"Not sure what she has against that glass." Della heaved a sigh. This wasn't the way she wanted to start her morning. "Looks like we lost the catering job."

Her mother came around the corner and hugged her. "Don't worry, sweetie. We're the last caterer in town she tried. All the others already dropped her. As for the tri-state region, let me say gossip travels fast and besides, no decent caterer would take her. If nothing else, we keep the deposit and order no more food. We keep what we have and use it for someone else's shindig. It's a win-win situation."

Maybe. Still, Della felt she shouldn't give up on finding Jeffrey Lawson. Someone needed to give him a heads up. It could be he had no clue he was neck-deep in software legal issues. "I think I'll keep working at Lawson Industries if you can handle the shop portion."

Her mother dropped her arms, stepped back, and grinned. "No worries, sweetie. I'm a people person. It keeps me abreast of the local gossip, especially when the legal clerks and paralegals visit."

Her eyebrows arched at the possibility of employees casually discussing cases with whomever they encountered. "What about confidentiality?"

A hearty chuckle sounded. "They aren't talking *at* me, but I'm a pretty good listener. It's all part of being the gossip hotline. Besides, it's my town, and I should know what's going on."

Della agreed with her mother's viewpoint. "Just make sure to keep your ears open for anything that might be pertinent."

"Always. I'm surprised you're working at Lawson's today."

"Me, too." Her shoulders went up in a shrug. "People want to complain on the weekend just as much as on a weekday. At least I have Sunday off. Since the bakery is closed, I'll have an actual day off. Can't wait."

Her mother patted her arm before she bustled behind the counter to inspect the coffee. "Not ready." She gave a little sigh. "I should have brought my own coffee, but yours is so good, even if I have to wait for it. You better finish up the cookies before you head out. You might even take some cookies to work. Gifts usually make people feel like they ought to reciprocate. Who knows? You might not get cookies, but possibly gain more trust. More trust, more information."

At this point, she'd grasp at what she could. Della grabbed a white bakery box and crammed it with scones, muffins, and cookies. When finished, she taped a business card to the top of the box. Right now, all she wanted was to find Lawson since the wedding reception probably died a fast death about five minutes ago. When she found him, she might warn him against Ellie. Her lips firmed as she considered the matter. One woman warning against another just came off as sounding petty. The best she could hope for was that common sense triumphed for a change.

CHAPTER THIRTEEN

THE SWEET TREATS made Della popular, even attracting strag- glers from other departments. Snippets of conversations reached her ears, including complaints about a spouse who didn't help—making the complainer late for work—bragging about a child's school project, and the occasional work reference. There was nothing about Lawson, though, and where he might be.

All the same, the compliments on the bakery goodies lightened her mood. At one point, she wondered if her head grew the tiniest little bit. She thanked everyone and managed to mention the name of her bakery at least three times—any more would have been excessive. Too bad she hadn't thought of extra business cards. The impromptu coffee break ended when only crumbs remained in the box. Todd, the guy Della met on the first day, wet his finger to pick up the minuscule morsels.

The sound of clapping caused the remaining employees to push away from the conference table. Della nodded in her boss's direc- tion. "If you like, I can bring more."

"Please do," Tyesha answered. "Only next time carry them in a plain paper box to fool everyone. I'm sure you meant those just for *our* department."

Her motivation leaned more toward people blabbing what they knew about Lawson and anything odd that might be an issue. What she got instead were inquiries about her different types of muffins and scones, along with a request for cookie bar information which forced her to tear off the slightly soiled business card from the box to hand over. Taking a page from her mother's book of eavesdropping, she discovered Jaime had had another date with her mystery man and a data entry employee had issues with her car and needed a new mechanic. Someone in shipping had a cat that just had kittens, and she passed around her phone to show off the little darlings. What no one said a single word about was their missing boss.

The four of them made their way to their desks. Lori kept close to Jaime, but her voice carried. "Where did he take you?"

Jaime grinned. "We went to a sushi bar in Centerville, and then we headed to a jazz club."

"Ooh…" Lori lengthened the word and turned to smirk at the two of them. "He sounds like a real hipster."

"Ha!" Tyesha snorted the word. "First of all, I can safely say there are no hipsters here. Secondly, they'd be listening to independent rock with weird names. Jazz is mainstream. So is sushi. All the same, it sounds like a good date. Right, Della?"

The fact her boss included her put a bounce into her step, which almost made her miss an opportunity to comment. "Ah, sounds like fun."

"It was," Jaime admitted with a shy face and a slight blush.

Not sure why today would merit more complaints, but they could hear the phones before they even turned the corner. Who was she kidding? The complaint calls never stopped. Not once did someone call to say how happy they were with their software. Happy people never called.

They slid into their seats and donned their headsets rather like knights getting ready for the crusades. Neither cause ranked as noble, but at least no one would get killed on her shift.

Lori's overloud response carried. "Yes, Stephanie, I do realize you called before. I may have even spoken to you."

Whoever was speaking at the other end couldn't see Lori's eye-rolls or her miming choking herself. "No ma'am, there's no patch to fix your program. It is what it is. Let me send you to the Technical Department."

Della could feel Lori's stare. She wanted Della to ask, so she did. "Who was that?"

The chair creaked as Lori spun it around. Her face took on an animated expression with wide-open eyes, including Lori framing the sides of her face with her hands. "Oh, my goodness! It was our number one caller."

Jaime pushed her mic away from her face to participate in the conversation. "Was it Stephanie?"

"You hit the target," Lori said as she shaped her thumb and forefinger into a gun and pointed it at her fellow employee. "If you're curious, I think it was her eighth—no, make that her thirty-eighth, or maybe her three hundredth call. It's hard to keep track despite telling me every time what number call it is." She threw her hands up, exasperated at trying to count. "The latest disaster wasn't that the software didn't create the slender, glamorous image the advertisement promised. She's called on that one before. No, this time, she said she picked the least offensive photo for the dating app, which the software automatically syncs to, and it uploaded the worst one as if it had a mind of its own."

A few days had already taught Della that very little got accomplished by contacting Customer Support Advantage. In some ways,

she felt guilty for taking money for not solving any issues. Technically, she hadn't gotten a paycheck yet. Surely that woman realized after
her first half dozen calls that nothing would get resolved. "Why does
she keep calling when nothing ever happens?"

Both women stared at her with arched brows and matching
offended expressions. Della gulped, realizing she'd basically said
none of them did anything of merit all day. "Ah, I mean, we all listen
and that's a plus. It could be that's all any of them really want."

An uncomfortable silence hung over the three of them until
Jaime giggled. "Don't look so horrified. We know we aren't doing
much right now. It's that stupid Glamorize program. It's not a
Lawson product. Not sure where it came from, but I guess we're now
promoting third party products which we know nothing about.
That's why everything goes to Tech. Apparently, they don't know
any more than we do, so they let the phone ring. Most of the time, if
it *were* a Lawson product, we could easily talk a person through the
program. We didn't get all that many calls because most of the
software was used by corporations who understood how it worked.
If there was a problem, they had an IT person to solve it, although
occasionally, we get calls from IT people asking for help."

Lori shook her head in acknowledgment and sniffed. "Before
Glamorize, we actually had enough people for the department."

Obviously, none of them knew the program had been hijacked,
stolen, or whatever you do when you take someone's intellectual
properties. As far as she could tell, it didn't work as advertised and
caused a backlash of customer complaints. It was hard to know why
Lawson even bothered with it. "Who suggested the program? Why
did they market it?"

The women looked at each other and shrugged.

Lori's mouth twisted one way, then the other. "Who knows? We're just peons. No one tells us anything. I imagine whoever came peddling this crappy software said something about making tons of money. Maybe they said it would make Lawson Industries an overnight success."

"Yeah, I can see that." Della could see people doing things for money and fame. "You sure Lawson didn't have anything to do with creating it?"

Jaime grimaced and reached back to rub her neck. "Our research and development department is a bunch of nerds who design software for insurance companies, accounting software, and educational games. They do not create makeover programs for photos. It's not their style."

"Odd. It makes me wonder where it came from," Della pondered aloud. "There's already a ton of software that changes how you look. Even my phone does that to an extent. Not too well, though. Once, when I clicked on a button to make me taller, I ended up looking like an alien. What is the appeal of this program?"

"Cheap, relatively speaking." Jaime's nose wrinkled as she answered. "If it were super cheap, people wouldn't complain about it. They'd forget about it like a bad fast-food meal, vowing never to visit that restaurant again, but after a couple of months when they can't recall their previous experience, they return. People's memories get better the more money they spend on something."

Della never bothered too much with photo enhancement. First, it never turned out without looking odd. To get good, enhanced images took folks with much more experience than she had. The big daddy in photo enhancement cost about two hundred dollars or more, and it had all these add-ons. Now, instead of a CD, people had to stream it and pay monthly fees. Whatever you wanted was never included, which was probably why a bunch of imitators popped up with lower prices. "What's too much money?"

Before Jaime could answer, Lori did with a sage bob of her head. "It depends on the person and their level of desperation. People pulling down a good salary wouldn't blink at a hundred dollars. Fifty dollars stings for a person just getting by. Glamorize is $69.99, which is in the sting zone, especially since it doesn't seem to be delivering on its promises." One hand fisted on her hip as she pursed her lips. "Maybe people who know how that stuff works could create the image they need, but it's sold to the general public, which means some of the same people who can't figure out why their unplugged computer isn't working, bought it."

"It would make sense just to drop the item, especially if it isn't making money." Della tended to be a big fan of the simplest method. "Why bother with it?"

"Contracts," Lori acknowledged with one word.

Jaime adjusted her headset, getting ready to return to her chiming phone, but tacked on, "Anna in accounting told me profits were up. Way up. All a person must do is buy the product once. Even if they hate it, they still have it. Open software can't be returned."

That much Della knew. Her thoughts drifted to the determined caller. "Has Stephanie threatened you or the company?"

A thoughtful mien came over Lori's countenance as she tapped a nail against her cheek. "No. Never. It's the usual drill. She tells me what number her call is and the product she is calling about that is at fault. Something like, this is my thirtieth call, and your lack of customer service is sadly lacking, or today was an upload issue. I say I'm sorry before sending her to tech support. Doesn't strike me as dangerous, just exasperated but determined. Don't make the mistake of wishing her a nice day."

Such a comment would bite since the consumer wasn't having a great day, and Lawson Industries might have played a part in it. "She's not dangerous?" Della said the words aloud, trying to formulate if the woman could be a threat.

"Far from it," Lori said with a smirk. "If the woman was some sort of mad bomber bent on revenge, it's no secret where Lawson industries are located." She pressed her hands together, and then pulled them apart, mimicking an explosion. "Boom! We'd all be history."

A valid point, but the memory of the single name of Stephanie in the daily agenda book stuck in her mind. Still, there had to be more than one person named Stephanie in this town.

Della cleared her throat. "Do you think if Lawson found out about your number one complainer, he might feel the need to address the issue personally?"

"Don't know." Lori reached back and rubbed her neck, and then moved the headphones over her ears, signaling the conversation was over. Jaime spun her chair and moved the mic away from her face to reply. "I can see him doing that. He's more of a hands-on guy than his father was. Last I heard, Lawson senior was off on some luxurious vacation. He probably doesn't even know his son is missing in action. Then again, he might know the real reason his son isn't showing up for work."

All Della needed to do was talk to the senior Lawson or the determined caller Stephanie.

CHAPTER FOURTEEN

MAIL LITTERED THE stainless-steel bakery counter. A few bore the unhappy message *Second Notice.* Della sighed. Whatever happened to the first notice? Could be most businesses considered paying on time as first notices. She picked up the bills and stared at them, hoping they'd magically transform into a check or even a congratulatory letter announcing that her guess at the number of jellybeans at the local Apple Blossom Festival would net her a long weekend at Branson. She closed her eyes and inhaled deeply. When she opened them, the electric bill with the threatening stamp still existed, along with the water bill.

Mabel's upbeat chatter carried back into the kitchen. Her mother had brought the mail in and saw the instruments of her dream's destruction and yet, she sounded as chipper as usual. It could be she didn't have her readers on or thought Della had simply forgotten to pay it. Curiosity brought her to the door for a peek. Instead of Ethan, a middle-aged man with a genial face and a generous waistline that challenged his shirt's expansion ability chatted with her mother.

Though Della couldn't place him right away, there was something familiar about him. The man leaned against the counter in Mabel's direction, causing his shirt to ride up. The position struck a responsive chord. Give the man a ball cap, stick him under the hood of a car, and you had Horace, the family mechanic.

Her mother must have heard her because she called out. "Might as well come in and thank Horace for what a great job he did on your car!"

Geesh. Della loved her mother but didn't appreciate being treated like she was eight years old. All the same, she pasted a smile on her face before pushing the door wide. "Hello, Horace. My car is working great now. Thanks so much."

Horace sniffed, and then inhaled audibly. "I've got to be honest with you. It's an old car. There's only so much I can do. There comes a time when you can no longer repair a car. It's almost impossible to get parts unless you hang out at the junkyard. Even that's dicey because people need to be junking cars like yours. Most have already scrapped their models years ago."

"Ah, thanks," Della mumbled, even though thankful wasn't what she felt. Somehow, Horace managed to make her feel worse than she already did. Everything rested on money or her lack of it. Ambition, hard work, or the ability to make a feather-light croissant didn't counteract being so deep in the red that she might as well function as a corpuscle.

Her mother reached across the counter to playfully tap Horace's arm as the two chattered about something that happened decades ago in grammar school. Such behavior by anyone else might be considered flirty—not her mother, though. She'd been more than clear about her ambivalent feelings about dating. Obviously, Horace and her mother attended the same school, which explained their camaraderie and ease with each other. Add to that, numerous successfully repaired vehicles, which endeared Horace to her mother.

Della's lips pursed as she noticed the flush on her mother's cheeks and Horace doing his best to suck in his belly but failing. A spark existed between the two. A possible romance distracted her from money issues for a few seconds.

A bell on the front door chimed, pulling Della from her contemplation of how her mother's life might change with a new man in it. Downtown Owens didn't offer much in after-hours activities, which equaled few to no customers after five pm—perhaps someone wanting a latte or a scone. More likely it was someone who wanted to use the bathroom. Maybe she should put up a sign about restrooms being for customers only.

Instead of a visitor with a full bladder, Ethan Stone filled the doorway. A street light's illumination outlined his broad shoulders and glinted on his hair. The open door allowed a chill to slither into the shop, as well. A less generous person might think he held the door open on purpose as an attention-getting device. Della rejected the idea. A man as ruggedly handsome as Ethan naturally received attention from both genders, although not all of it good.

His eyes roamed the almost empty shop. When he saw Della, he grinned. "Just the person I want to see."

That, she seriously doubted. Della drifted to the coffee urn, certain there had to be some of her secret blend left. It would also explain his late visit. "Coffee?"

"Sure." He moved into the room, pulling the door closed behind him. "I never say no to a cup of Joe. What I really need to do is talk to you. Remember at the singles mixer I said we needed to talk?"

Two fingers went up in a modified gesture that combined a salute and a wave as he passed her mother. "Hello, Mabel."

"Hey, Good Lookin'," her mother answered, pulling a frown

from Horace.

Her remark caused Ethan to chuckle as he took a seat at the table nearest the window. He cut his eyes to Della and patted the chair next to him. Cocky. Did he expect her to deliver coffee and possibly a snack to his table? Worse yet, would he be like Kyle and expect everything to be on the house since she owned the bakery? Well, she'd toss the coffee in a couple of minutes, so that wouldn't be too big of a waste.

Della poured two cups and carried them to the table. "So, what do we have to talk about?" As far as she knew, she didn't have any information about the missing heir.

He thanked her for the coffee and took the proffered cup, blew on it, sipped, and then added with a smirk, "Old, but better than coffee left on the burner at other places."

As compliments went, it wasn't the best. "Thanks, I think."

His attitude had certainly taken a turn for the worse. Maybe he was tired and possibly frustrated at his lack of progress on the case. That had to be it.

"Find out anything about Lawson?" Ethan asked as he scrolled through his phone, not even making eye contact.

Not exactly the image of a man who was interested in what she had to say. Perhaps he had guessed she didn't really know anything. All the same, she should say something. "Cheap."

"Huh?" Ethan glanced up from his phone. "What do you mean?"

"That's what I hear around Lawson Industries. Apparently, some of the office equipment is ancient. Rumor is nothing gets replaced until it breaks."

"Okay. Sounds like most CEOs." He rested his elbow on the table, then cradled his chin in his upraised hand. His lips lifted into a smile. "You're a smart girl. See anything else?"

She was a smart *woman*. So far, she hadn't been too impressed with Ethan's skills, even though there was no reason for him to tell her what he'd found so far. Her eyes narrowed, and her lips twisted to one side as she tried to recall their backroom conversation at the singles speed date. The general impression leaned toward shared information. At best, he might be looking for confirmation on what he already knew. Della summed it up in one word. "No."

No reason to mention the datebook. It might come to nothing. All she did was hang around some potted plants and took shots of a cryptic planner, along with somehow re-igniting Kyle's interest. Della shifted restlessly in her seat, pondering if padded seats would be beneficial to her business. Would people stay longer and buy more, or would they just sit around and nurse a single cup of java all day?

Her mother's shriek of laughter had Della twisting in her chair. Whatever they were talking about was more fun than being half-heartedly questioned about Lawson. A warm hand covered hers, forcing Della's head to snap back so fast she resembled a dashboard bobblehead doll in a demolition rally.

"Ah…" She stumbled about for words, then cut her eyes to his larger hand encompassing hers rather like a shell covering a penny in a con game. The idea of being part of a con game reminded her of the nefarious sorts lurking about. "Have any trouble with those thugs?"

His resting hand gave hers a little squeeze before its departure due to Ethan kicking back his chair on two back legs. Della squeezed her eyes shut, expecting an inevitable crunch as the chair collapsed or at the very least, a tumble. Nothing.

Several trains of thought pulled into her mind-station, jostling to be first. What if there were never any thugs? It could be something Ethan made up to stop her from looking. The thought worked as a possibility.

Before she could become too entrenched in the first idea, a second idea tooted its own whistle. Even tired, Ethan radiated charm and sex appeal, rather like one of those 1950s movie stars without the period clothing. Her eyebrows arched as she considered the man. Along with being good looking, he never tired of asking her questions. An easy way to throw someone off the track was to mention a bogeyman while never saying who it was.

The wall supported the back of the flimsy chair, saving Ethan from an embarrassing fall. He tucked his hands behind his neck and stared up at the ceiling. "You've got nothing to worry about with me here."

What was he? A human shield? Was he able to throw up a force field that none could penetrate? A quick survey of the man reminded her of all the reasons she considered him to be honest and hardworking when they first met. It made her wonder if she should trust her initial impression.

"I've got to get things ready for closing if I want to get any sleep tonight."

Her announcement resulted in chair legs dropping and skittering a tiny bit across the tile floor before coming to a stop. Ethan blew out an exasperated breath. "Della, I'm trying to help you. You've got to believe me."

Help? She sucked her lips in to prevent an impulsive outburst. The more tired she was, the more likely she'd say what she thought—another little quirk that didn't endear her to anyone. So far, all the man had done was pump her for information. Most of the time, he'd been charming, not too hard on the eyes, and not hurting her reputation to be seen talking with him.

Ethan might even believe what he was saying. Not so with Della. She didn't know much about private investigators, but she assumed they were more efficient than Ethan. It could be he was only pretending to investigate. Her father used to call investigators wannabe detectives—hopeless amateurs who didn't have a clue how things worked unless they were retired law enforcement, and then they were okay.

She wasn't giving the man any more information since he had given her nada that she trusted thus far. Sharing worked both ways. It could be he had nothing to share, or more likely, he had no intention of exchanging information. The latter would make him a spoilsport. It could also mean he might be the thug he'd warned her about.

CHAPTER FIFTEEN

T HE BELL ON the bakery door clanged as Ethan closed the door. Even the bell refused to participate in its normally cheery jingle as if it, too, had somehow been deceived by the man. Della crossed her arms, slumped in her chair, and glared at the closed door. She hadn't asked Ethan if he was engaged. Her mother, who wasn't known for her tact, had asked if he was married. While his answer had been *no* with a wide, toothy grin, he missed the opportunity to say *soon to be married.*

Her fingers rubbed her neck as she replayed the scene. Even though her mother served as an official cheerleader for Ethan, Della had turned in her pom-poms long before this last meeting. All this grilling her about what she knew and all he offered was a paltry compliment or two, which some women might consider flirting. On a few occasions, she might have been one of those women.

Sure, he could have worked as a model for some athletic wear company that featured bearded guys ready to scale a mountain face or step into a canoe to explore an uncharted river. It reminded her of one of her grandmother's many sayings—*Pretty is as pretty does.* It had baffled her, so she'd asked for an explanation. Always concise, her gentle nana said, "Good looks aren't enough." Not enough for her and a hunch something wasn't quite right made for a disastrous coffee date even before he dropped the bomb.

Ethan had glanced down at his phone when a notification sounded, read the text, and was half-standing before he even spoke. "Emergency back home. I need to go check on my fiancée."

The man didn't even wait for her acknowledgment. He shrugged his jacket on and left. It could be the emergency centered on extra-large shrimp the caterer couldn't find. Something serious could have happened, such as a car wreck, since she doubted few women were as big of a diva as Ellie. Then, there was the possibility Ethan *didn't* have a fiancée. He expected that the mention of the woman back home would dash any plans Della had made regarding the two of them.

If he'd asked, she could have told him her mother would be more upset not to have him hanging around than Della would. Knowing Mabel, she probably already imagined tiny Ethan's, minus the beard, running around.

As if knowing she was needed, her mother exited the kitchen, wiping her hands on a dishtowel. Her head pivoted one way, then another. Finally, she stood on her toes and peered over the counter at the floor as if she'd find Ethan flattened against the tile for some bizarre reason.

"Where did he go?"

No need to mention who she meant since Della and Ethan had been the only two people in the shop area. "Oh, you know," Della shrugged her shoulders. "Something about rushing home to see his fiancée."

"His what!" Mabel slapped the counter before she marched into the seating area. Her fisted hands found purchase on her hips as she gave the place a thorough survey as if the man in question had somehow melted into the wall.

The lack of Ethan in the general vicinity should be obvious. Della felt the need to emphasize it, though. "I'm sure he's in his car by now heading back to wherever home is." Her mouth twisted to one side as she considered the other possibility. "Either that or he told me that to kill any interest I might have in him. Mention of a fiancée or wife tends to throw cold water on a budding relationship."

A derisive snort answered her comment. Her mother pulled out the chair Ethan had recently vacated and sat down. "I thought I knew the man. People tell me I'm a good judge of men. I would have sworn he was interested in you."

Actions speak louder than words and his had practically shouted. Della settled for another shrug. "It doesn't matter. At first, he acted as if he might like me, but then it seemed all he ever did was pump me for information. It's not like I know much, but I quit telling him what I did know. Then, poof." She snapped her fingers.

"Ah, I see." Mabel gave a sage nod. "You're better off without him."

There was no reason to point out that she never had him to begin with. A person couldn't lose what they never had. And there was no reason for her not to move onto the next step of her search, and interview the frequent caller, Stephanie, who shared the same name as the appointment in Lawson's planner. Thank goodness the woman made a habit of stating her full name, which would be recorded in Lori's log book. Each customer service representative had to record the time of each call and the name of the caller. Occasionally, you get someone who rant for a good ten minutes, even questioning the rep's parentage, but in the end refused to give a name. They were logged as anonymous, although the reps have other, more appropriate names for them.

All she needed to do was peek in Lori's log book or simply ask.

DELLA SHUFFLED HER feet as she peered at the modest vinyl siding house in front of her. A few plastic sunflowers brightened the front, even though they appeared rather incongruous surrounded by fallen leaves. She bit her lip as she pondered her next move. Why was she still on the trail of Jeffrey Lawson?

Both she and her mother expected the wedding to be a lost cause, but not because Ellie had threatened to get another caterer at the last minute. No one would dare take her on, especially without her fiancé footing the bill. The missing bridegroom would be the issue. Unlike the movies, Ellie didn't have anyone to take her latest beau's place.

A diamond-shaped space appeared in the blinds as the current resident peered out to see who lingered on her doorstep. *Great.* Della needed to do something or she'd appear odd. A glance at the notecard on which she'd scrawled Stephanie's name and address gave the appearance of purpose. If she'd brought a box with her, she could have at least pretended to be delivering something. Delivery people seldom talked to the package's intended recipient, which wouldn't serve her. Stephanie came as close to a lead as she had— more of a hunch than a lead, but what else did she have?

One foot in front of the other, she prompted herself as she made her way to the door. All the usual reasons people rang your doorbell wouldn't work, especially with her inability to lie. Too bad Ethan Stone wasn't here. Apparently, that man had no issues with lying or not telling the entire truth. The topic of his fiancée never came up until yesterday. Della's lips pulled tight as she ground her back molars. Why had she listened to her mother? Her well-meaning parent mentioned make-up might not hurt, especially if she knew Ethan would drop by.

A fat lot of good that did her. The heat from the convection oven had made her eyeliner sweat and smear giving her the appearance of a soon-to-be victim in a horror flick. Unfortunately, this small detail became apparent when she ducked into the bathroom after her coffee meeting and beheld her frightening visage. The man had never thought of her in a romantic fashion. Instead, he expected her to provide information garnered from Lawson Industries free of charge.

"Stupid!" She growled the word and stomped the final steps to the door. Inhaling deeply, she tried to focus on the matter at hand. Ethan had hightailed it out of the area while assuring Della the police would find the missing heir. Weird, especially since he had seemed so determined earlier. So far, not a lot had happened on the police front. No foul play was suspected, and everyone knew Ellie could be demanding. It could be they thought Lawson got cold feet, which oddly, Della didn't. No ransom was demanded, which ruled out kidnapping. Her time at Lawson Industries informed her that Lawson was a hard worker who paid his workers a fair wage, if not a luxurious one, which ruled out disgruntled employee for the most part.

Her hand fisted, ready to knock, when the door flew open, revealing a female on the downside of thirty. She narrowed her eyes.

"I don't know you. What are you doing here?" She threw the words as if aiming at a carnival game with Della serving as the target.

Her plan to pretend being lost in order to strike up a conversation quickly vanished. Besides, almost everyone had GPS on their phones. "Ah…"

She swallowed hard. Ethan had confided he stuck as close to the truth as possible when soliciting info. It made it easier since he didn't have to remember a convoluted story. Maybe she should do likewise.

Della held up her card. "You're Stephanie Majewski."

"I am," the woman grudgingly admitted and peered around Della. "Is it just you?"

It wasn't exactly what she wanted to hear. "I'm here on behalf of Lawson Industries Customer Advantage."

"Customer Advantage?" The woman echoed the words. "What's that?"

"Customer Service."

"You've got precious little of that! I know. I've called several times only to have my call transferred to nowhere. It just rang and rang until I hung up. One time, I waited two hours, and then someone picked up the phone and immediately hung up. Rude!"

Her fellow employee, Jaime, had suspicions that the tech guys ignored the calls. Why else would the same people keep calling? Stephanie had earned herself the title of the number one complainer. Each time she called, she said her name and how many times she had called previously.

"That's why I'm here. It's come to my attention that the Tech Department's phones may not be working correctly."

"Yeah." She gave a derisive snort. "My phone tends not to work either when someone's on the other end I don't want to talk to."

"I'm here now, ready to listen to your issue and see what I…" She stopped herself, wondering if she was using the right pronoun for soothing the irate individual. Maybe not. "…*we* can work out."

Stephanie had her hand on the door and a scowl on her face. "Too little, too late."

The door inched forward. Della considered putting her foot in the opening but rejected it as soon as she thought of it. She didn't want to find Lawson bad enough to have her foot slammed in the door. "Wait! How about a full refund?"

A few inches remained from total closure when the door stopped. Stephanie pulled it back open and asked with a skeptical expression. "Full refund? Do I have to buy the newest version of Glamorize, which costs twice as much? The last version I bought cost me plenty and didn't deliver on any of its promises."

It didn't take a psychologist to read Stephanie's crossed arms and mulish expression. "That's why I'm here." Her hand slipped into her purse to retrieve a pen and clicked it. "What promises do you mean?"

Stephanie snorted. "You should know. Don't you work for Lawson Industries?"

"I do." She forced a smile. "I'm a recent employee." Della giggled. "I know I should know, but I don't. If you don't mind, could you tell me your exact complaints? Once I type your answers into the survey spreadsheet, a check for a full refund will be mailed to you."

Stephanie's mouth twisted to one side as she pondered the possibility. The sound of something falling in the distance caused her to wince and step outside, closing the door behind her. "Dog," she explained with a grimace.

"I love dogs." Della spoke without considering how it might fit into her plan. "Can I see it? My dog, Snoopy, died a few years ago. I haven't had the heart to get a new dog since."

"Dogs are a lot of work." Stephanie gave her head a hard shake. Her eyes rolled upward as if remembering. "My dog was a rescue and must have been a street dog. Very aggressive. No wonder he was in the shelter."

"Nice of you to take him." Della waggled her pen as she analyzed the dog story. Most people, no matter how badly behaved their pet is, still gushed about it. "Getting back to the purpose of my visit—you said Glamorize didn't keep its promises?"

"Not in the least." Stephanie held up an index finger. "It was supposed to remove years off an image. All I got was a smooth, plastic appearance. Rather like those bad avatars you see on social media."

"Mm…" Della acknowledged as she wrote *younger image looks fake*. "I can see how that wouldn't work. Anything else?"

"You better believe it." She brandished two fingers and waved them. "The slimmer selection is just as bad as the younger one. With that my body remained plus size, but my face narrowed, almost like looking into a funhouse mirror. Not good."

Geesh. Didn't anyone test this software? Not surprisingly, it had disappointed her mother, too. Even though she hated to ask, Della felt she should. "Ok, are there any other issues?"

A muffled pounding penetrated the door. Stephanie bit her lip, cast an anxious look over her shoulder, and muttered, "Red eyes, green skin. Can I get my check today?"

Talk about a snag in her not fully thought-out plan. Della cleared her throat. "I'll submit your claim as soon as I return to the office. It should be less than a week, being a local address and all."

"Good!" Stephanie proclaimed, slipped inside, shut the door, and locked it.

Rude, but she was just upset. Della represented Lawson Industries, a company that represented disappointment and obvious fraudulent advertising. There was nothing to do but walk away, certain Stephanie had an eye on her. She might even have one of those motion-activated cameras.

Talking about dogs made her think about her own deceased darling. She'd had Snoopy for more than half of her life. While the boxer mix excelled at escaping from cages, fences, and pretty much any form of containment, he had never, ever knocked on a door.

CHAPTER SIXTEEN

W HAT NEXT? DELLA sat in her car, still parked in Stephanie's neighborhood, pondering her encounter with the enigmatic woman. Most people who call to complain would be excited to have their money refunded. While Stephanie okayed the idea of a check coming her way, she wasn't ecstatic despite calling Lawson Industries endlessly. Maybe she didn't want the money back, but would rather have the software work as promised. A sharp bark pierced her reverie.

An elderly woman was walking a small, hairy dog of indeterminate parentage on a long leash. The canine charged toward Della's car, yapping all the way. Not able to control the energetic dog, the owner shot Della a narrow-eyed look as if she were the cause of the dog's bad manners. Another nearby resident stopped clipping his bushes to peer in the direction of the hubbub. When it looked like the man might join the angry dog woman, Della decided to leave and started the car.

It wasn't like she was doing anything wrong, technically. Della did work for Lawson Industries and handled complaints. The personal visit and promising a refund were all on her. At first, she viewed it as the perfect ploy to talk to Lawson Industries' most frequent caller. The only problem, besides Della giving her actual name, was Stephanie would expect a refund and would call endlessly if she didn't get one, possibly mentioning the house call. Even though Della squeezed every cent until it screamed and kicked, she'd have to cough up the money for the refund herself. There was no way she could get anyone in Lawson Industries to write a check, and putting cash in an unmarked envelope would look too much like a drug drop. That last thing she needed was to attract the wrong kind of attention.

Her modest compact moved carefully through the neighborhood with Della doing her best not to attract any more attention. Depending on the residents, driving under the speed limit might be suspicious. A grandfather searching for his grandson driving slowly through her mother's neighborhood got reported as a suspicious person. Still, all the same, to speed up now could be viewed as unusual, too. While her car might be creeping through the neighborhood, her mind raced.

Where could she trim non-existent financial fat to be able to pay the promised refund? Real companies usually just gave store credit as opposed to refunding money. Then there was the issue of Stephanie, who didn't act as she expected. However, truthfully, Della had never taken a call from her, which meant she had no baseline for behavior. Even so, the woman's actions leaned toward anxious with a touch of peculiar, and what was with all that knocking?

The neighborhood street exited onto one of the main thoroughfares, which gave Della the opportunity to tap the accelerator. Owens started as a small town with one-way streets and the occasional two-lane street. As it grew, the best they could do was add various vanishing lanes for turning and merging. Della slid into one of the added lanes. Her rearview mirror revealed no sign of an approaching car, except one far in the distance, which would be no issue with the thirty-miles-per-hour speed limit.

The knocking bothered her. What if Stephanie held Jeffrey Lawson captive in her basement as revenge for non-functioning software? Crazy. Who did that? More likely it was an off-balanced washing machine making the thumping noise. Della clicked her turn signal on before merging because that's who she was—a rule follower.

An intuitive nudge had her checking her mirror again only to find an expensive sedan barreling down on her. Della yanked the steering wheel hard to the right, bumping up over the curb and tearing across a smooth, green lawn as the speeding vehicle veered into her former lane. Della stopped her car, pressed her hand against her chest, and stared after the reckless driver's car. Not a brake light in sight as it sped away. It all happened so fast. She pulled in a deep breath, trying to slow down her heart.

Della blinked a couple of times and then exhaled. For the briefest moment, she saw a determined female behind the wheel when she glanced in the mirror. The grim line of the lips had Della reacting reflexively, not stopping to think logically. It could be a drunk driver, but a memory of the severe expression dispelled the possibility. A colorful scarf hid the woman's hair, but something about the set visage struck a responsive chord.

A full-body shiver came over her. Della held onto the steering wheel until it passed. *Someone had it out for her.* That was a first for her. No history of stealing boyfriends, backstabbing co-workers, or stealing recognition for a job well done caused anyone to scratch threatening messages in her car's paint job or inspire hang-up phone calls, let alone trying to push her off the road.

It couldn't be Stephanie. There had been no time for her to get in her car, loop around the street, and then drive like a maniac and be ready to hit Della. Besides, why would she since Della had yet to issue a refund? It wasn't Stephanie's style. However, being able to declare what the woman might do based on a five-minute meeting probably wasn't appropriate sleuth work. Only a few moments before she had wondered if Stephanie had locked up the Lawson heir because of poorly performing software, rather like the character in the movie who kept a writer captive until he continued a series he had ended. All the same, the narrow face bore no resemblance to Stephanie's rounded one.

Her heartbeat returning to normal, Della opened her car door and exited the vehicle for a damage inspection. Slow, measured steps carried her around the car, which showed no obvious damage. She couldn't say the same for the lawn. Della felt like she should say something to the homeowner and turned to the front door. Certainly, they must have noticed a car on their front lawn by now.

Three steps led up to the front door where a heavy real estate lockbox commanded attention. Della glanced over her shoulder for a For Sale sign she must have missed. About eight feet from her car, half-hidden in the bushes was a broken sign. Apparently, she hadn't missed the sign at all.

A quick glance in the curtainless window revealed wood floors and moderately high ceilings with no furniture. At least no one was living there. The obvious car tire marks wouldn't be a selling point. There wasn't much she could do, but another glance at the broken sign told her which realtor she needed to call. Before leaving, Della propped the sign up against the house. It might not be the best advertising, but it was still advertising.

Nervous after such a close call, she drove under the speed limit as she wound her way back to the bakery. At each stop sign and stoplight, she checked her rearview mirror for speeding vehicles. Almost there, she reassured herself as if talking to a frightened child. The fanciful bakery sign brought her a measure of comfort as she turned into the alley to reach the back parking space. Maybe it had been all a fluke. Owens had its share of crazy drivers. As for the woman's angry expression, it could be the result of a hands-free phone call from a husband or boyfriend. A recent online article noted that angry drivers were just as dangerous, or more so than drunk drivers. Then again, what if the driver was one of the thugs Ethan had mentioned?

Della parked her car and switched off the ignition. Part of her had discarded the thug story as a way of Ethan's extracting information from her without doing any of the legwork. While that could be true, what if there were actual thugs, or possibly an assassin, sent out to either find or eliminate Jeffrey Lawson? No one ever expected a woman when it came to crime. Well, make that they only expected a woman when it came to her husband. Before she could analyze why a thug would be after her, Mabel came flying out the back door, waving her hands.

"You won't guess what happened while you were gone!"

Good Heavens! Did Della even want to know?

CHAPTER SEVENTEEN

D ELLA SHOULDERED HER purse and slammed the car door while
absorbing the appearance of her beaming mother standing
bare-armed outside the back door of the bakery. A chilly breeze
slipped through the alley and as if playing tag, making a point to
touch everyone standing.

"Mom!" She strolled to the door to encourage her mother to go
inside. "No reason to discuss this outside. What has you all smiles?"

"Wait!" Mabel grabbed Della's arm. "Don't go inside yet."

The ominous words stopped all forward movement. Had the
health inspector showed up unannounced? Technically, they were
always supposed to do so, but if you knew someone, and her mother
did, you could get a heads up to do a little extra cleaning. For the
most part, the bakery gleamed. Still, from her short stint working at
Baby Cakes bakery, she knew inspectors could be picky. One fined
the business because the coils on the fridge compressor were dusty.
Della knew they had been cleaned because she had done it, but
apparently, not good enough.

"Health inspectors?"

"What?" Her mother's penciled in eyebrows drew together.
"There are no health inspectors."

At least something had worked out in her favor. She glanced
down at her mother's hand still gripping her arm. "What's got you

so excited?"

"Well." Her mother cleared her throat, glanced back toward the door, and lowered her voice before continuing, "Horace asked me out."

"Really?" Della emphasized the word. This was surprising, especially since her mother blew all hot and cold about the prospect of dating. It would do her mother good to get out and have some fun. "I assume you said yes."

"Oh, no." She shook her head. "When I saw you drive by, I came out immediately to ask your opinion."

Wait a minute. That meant—Della reached for the door, dragging her mother with her. "Is Horace still inside?"

"I think so." Mabel wrinkled her nose. "I hope so. Do you think he may have taken me dashing out of the room as an answer of some type?"

Her mother *really* had been out of the dating game for a long time. While Della was no expert when it came to dating, she was certain running out of the room might be construed negatively. "He should know you by now. Let's go inside and see if he's still here."

"You're right." Mabel agreed and shivered. "It's too cold to stay out here. What do you think I should do?"

Della tamped down her first impulse to encourage her mother to go out, even though her mother might be happier having a gentleman friend to fuss over. "What do *you* want to do?"

"Right now, get back inside." The two of them hustled into the warm back room where the residual smell of cinnamon and chocolate hung in the air. Mabel patted her hair. "Okay, here goes nothing."

Even though Della wouldn't mind being the proverbial fly on the wall, she hung back in the kitchen. Everyone deserved privacy. It would be dating baby steps. She already knew Horace and possibly some of his peculiarities, such as telling the same lame jokes repeatedly, possibly encouraged by customers who forced out a chuckle to get their vehicles repaired at a reasonable price. Even though Della already decided to give her mother some room, she still found herself at the pass-through door, straining her ears to hear anything. The front doorbell jingled, giving her the perfect reason to enter the shop. After all, she *was* the owner.

Two of her co-workers waved as they entered the shop. Jaime nudged Lori. "See, I told you it was the right place."

"You did," Lori acknowledged and made her way up to the counter. "We're hoping to snag some of the goodies you brought to work. Got any of those pumpkin muffins?"

Since the muffins tended to be oversized and cost twice as much as the regular muffins, Della usually opted for making only a dozen a day. A quick glance at the display case revealed the inventory situation. "I'm afraid not. They go quick this time of year." That might have been stretching it a bit since the bakery had only been open a few months and she had nothing to compare her sales against. Della gestured to the bottom case. "Would you care to sample an orange scone, lemon drop cookie, or a bear claw?"

"Hmm," Lori peered into the case. "They all look good."

Jaime waved her hand as if refusing the suggestion. "I came for a chocolate croissant and a latte."

The words sent Della into action. She plated the croissant and heated it a tiny bit as she made the latte. Her mother and Horace had moved off to a table to continue their discussion, making it hard to eavesdrop.

"You know," Lori held up an index finger, "You could bring a box of goodies to work and sell them easily. Most of the workers are snacking out of the vending machines. That stuff must be a hundred years old."

The idea had merit. Even if she only sold a couple dozen it would still help her bottom line. "I don't know." She crouched to grasp the lemon drop cookie Lori pointed to with her plastic-gloved hand, "What about Mr. Lawson? Would he approve?"

"Hard to know with his not being there." Lori shrugged. "Coffee, too." Her lips twisted to one side. "Better make it decaf this late. Anyhow, the rumor is Lawson senior is cutting his trip short to run the business since Junior isn't around."

No one commented on it being odd that Jeffrey Lawson had disappeared. The subject had been talked to death at break time. The fact the older Lawson was flying in from Aruba or whatever exotic place he had been vacationing meant this was serious, not just cold feet from contemplating tying the knot.

After paying, Jaime angled her head at a nearby table. "Can you join us?"

"Sure," Della answered, glad for the lack of business that time of night. She picked up a plain, white stoneware cup, made herself a nutmeg latte, and carried it to the table. On one hand, she might be sliding down a financial ski slope, but she did get an invite to chat. Casual friendships she didn't do that well. It wasn't that she didn't like people. She did, but too much of her time went into trying to be the best she could at anything she did.

It hadn't always been this way, but a throwaway remark a fellow camper made at scout camp when she was eleven stayed with her. The other girl had a half-dozen siblings and acted confused that

Della had none. When she explained her parents had her late in life and there would be no other children, the fellow camper sighed and told her she'd have to be everything to her parents because they had no backup children. She'd have to be the brain, the athlete, the artist, *and* the beauty queen.

While Mabel worked on being the best mom, Della studied hard to be on the honor roll consistently. A few seasons in soccer demonstrated both a lack of skill and competitive drive, which killed the athlete role. Della would have settled for being a good student until she found baking. Being driven made her the opposite of a party girl.

Della did have some equally scholarly friends, Layne, and Celeste, who snagged scholarships for out-of-state schools, but never returned to Owens. Layne, her old lab partner, married a guy she'd met at college, which made her failure to return understandable. Celeste lived alone with her cat in the big city of Columbus, Ohio, seduced by the bright lights and art theatres that showed black and white foreign films with subtitles, along with the possibility of getting sushi twenty-four hours a day. The last caused Della's lips to twist into a sneer. Who'd want sushi when they could have a yummy éclair instead?

Latte in hand, she shot a curious glance at her mother's table and caught the words, miniature golf. They were planning a date. How sweet. A little cold to chase a ball around a colorful windmill or hit it into a green-carpeted volcano, but there was an inside range at the nearby mall in Clemmons.

She moved toward her friends and noticed they were both chewing. "What's the verdict?" she asked and slid into the closest empty chair.

"Delicious," Jaime offered with a grin.

Lori held up what was left of her cookie. "Very zesty. I love it. It's not one of those yellow cookies you need to be told is lemon. This cookie shouts its contents."

Normally, Della might have considered a shouting cookie a bad thing. If her co-worker's consumption served as an indicator, she needed more shouting cookies. "Okay, so, what's this about old Lawson returning?"

"Rumor." Lori reminded and waggled her eyebrows. "I heard it from Toby, who got it from Delean, who happens to be tight with Barbie. It's probably ninety percent true. I guess we'll know when he shows."

While Lori sipped her coffee, Jaime spoke as if they were like a wrestling tag team. "I wouldn't worry about senior. He keeps to his elevated floor. He won't be down to check on us peons. You could easily bring in your goodies. Lots of parents bring in order sheets for their kids' various sales. Make a general price and put out a jar for the money. Some people might stiff you but pay you the next day. A few might even pay over your asking price, thrilled to have something fresh and tasty for a change."

It might even help Della to make up the money she needed to give to Stephanie. "What does senior think happen to his son?"

Jaime drummed her nails on the table and grimaced. "As I said, he doesn't come down to our floor. We won't know until he gets here. Then we rely on Toby hanging around Delean to get a tidbit. Besides, it can't be too bad. The police would have been notified, or there would have been a ransom note. It could even be he's faking his own death to get out of marrying Ellie."

Faking your own death would be extreme, but some celebrities or those involved with celebrities had done so to escape relation-ships. Nevertheless, it didn't explain Ethan's presence or his sudden exit. So far, everyone believed the younger Lawson left on his own. That would mean he used his own car. If nothing else, she should at least check out his residence to see if his car remained. She knew what she'd be doing after work tomorrow.

Someone asked her a question or at least she thought they did because both co-workers had matching inquisitive expressions. "Excuse me. Could you repeat that? It's noisy in here." It wasn't.

"What are you doing tomorrow after work?" Jaime inquired with the slightest chin bob.

Admitting she planned to nib around the boss's house would not serve. Instead, she held out her hands. "I'm as free as a bird."

Mentally, she added, *if the bird was an overweight chicken with its wings clipped and had intentions of going where it shouldn't.*

CHAPTER EIGHTEEN

D ELLA CLANGED THE dirty mixing bowl against the side of the stainless-steel sink. It rang as if it were a singing bowl, but the discordant type that put your teeth on edge as opposed to being relaxing. Why did she agree to go to the movies with Jaime when she had so much to do, including finding Jeffrey Lawson?

The simple answer was it had been too long since she had done anything fun with a friend. The few ambush dinners where co-workers tried to match her up with a fellow single person were not fun. It must be what running the last mile of a marathon felt like when the exhausted runner knew the end existed somewhere in the future and had to mentally remind herself to keep picking up the feet and putting them down.

Somehow, she'd work it out. On one hand, it wasn't fair to her mother, who had spent most of her time in the bakery helping. The initial plan was once the bakery started making money, she'd hire someone. She was still waiting on the money to start pouring in so she could hire some teenager who wouldn't expect a huge paycheck or forty hours.

The back door opened, and her mother entered, humming a song about dancing from one of her favorite musicals, *The King and I*. Della knew most of the musicals. She used to watch them with her mother. Being the only child, her mother would ever have, she'd felt obliged to sit beside her and comment on the costumes, plot lines—usually predictable—and the lyrics, which were better than the plots. Over time, she gained some fondness for the shows, too.

Della stripped off her rubber gloves and danced over to her mother, grabbing her hand after she deposited her oversized tote on the work table, then waltzed her around the kitchen for a few turns. Winded, they both stopped, grinned at one another, and chuckled.

She nudged her mother. "Should I ask what has you in such a good mood?"

"You can." Her mother sang the words as she hung up her jacket on a hook beside the door. She slipped an apron emblazoned with the name of the bakery over her head. "Horace is such a gentleman. He let me win at miniature golf and bought me ice cream later."

"Sounds like a good date. Do you think Horace just might be bad at golf?" Della regretted saying it as soon as she did, but her logical mind tended never to accept the simplest solution. It just kept on digging.

Mabel smirked as she worked a hairnet over her curls. "No one could be that bad. It had to be an act. Then, when I totaled up the score, and he found out he'd lost, he pouted. Isn't that sweet?"

Pouting males never did anything for Della. The appeal of such expression probably wore thin about age five. Her mother saw the best in almost every situation. If she thought it was darling, then it was.

"I'm glad you had a good time. Um..." She hesitated, not willing to ask since her mother spent so much time helping her. *Helicopter parents* served as the term for parents who did too much for their children. Of course, that referred to young children, not adult children. "Never mind."

Her mother blinked and then shot her daughter a curious look. Aware of her inability to fabricate, Della turned back to the sink, turned on the water, and donned the gloves. The last thing she wanted to be was a subject of a letter to one of those self-help columnists nicknamed *Agony Aunts*. The letter might say something about devoting her life to raising her daughter, and she was still working to get her adult daughter on her feet. Nope, she didn't want that. Perhaps starting a bakery with little business background or experience hadn't been a smart thing to do.

The water stopped gushing into the sink as Mabel turned it off. "Come on. What were you going to say?"

"Doesn't matter."

"Does, too."

Her mother fixed her with the *mom* look. If crocodiles were female, it must have been the same stare they gave crocodile hunters before they latched onto their boots and refused to let go. Her mother had that type of tenacity.

She didn't have time for this. She planned on making extra goodies for work today. "It's no biggie. Jaime wanted me to go to some silly rom-com movie with her after work." She shrugged and crinkled her nose as if the possibility didn't entice.

"Great!" her mother replied enthusiastically. "You need to get out and have fun. This way I won't feel so guilty about going to dinner with Horace tonight, knowing you'll be doing something fun."

If her mother went out tonight, that meant there would be no one to watch the bakery for the half-dozen customers that might show. "Ah, forget about it. You go have fun. I'll stay at the bakery."

Her mother's nostrils flared as she took an audible breath. "Della

Marie Delacroix!"

For a moment, Della wondered, and not for the first time, why she never went by Marie. It certainly would have made her life much easier. Whenever the full name came out, it meant a parental lecture. What now? She gestured with her gloved hand for her mother to continue.

"You open up this store at seven am to take advantage of those heading to work."

Della nodded since this wasn't news to her. Her mother had to be going someplace with this. "Most bakeries and donut shops open that early and a few even open earlier."

Her mother held up her index finger, ready to make a point. "Exactly and the majority close by two o'clock in the afternoon."

That much Della knew to be true. "That's why I stay open in an effort to capture the late afternoon and evening business the other places aren't getting."

"You've told me this before, but did it ever occur to you there is no late afternoon or evening business? The downtown empties out around five. All the other stores keep banker's hours except for a couple of restaurants. Do you think people going to McLaren's Fish House or Yancy's Pub say to themselves, what I need is a decent coffee or an apricot pastry? They won't leave their current eating establishment to pop over here for something."

"It *could* happen." Her brow furrowed as she contemplated the scenario her mother drew. "Maybe more in the summer if we offered ice cream."

Her mother sniffed. "Right now, staying open forever on the off chance someone might stroll in is a waste of your time and re-sources. You have a definite opening time. Stick to a closing time such as four. Put big signs inside the shop about the new hours. Those who need a goodie after work can buy it on the way to work or during their lunch hour. These long hours are like a girl waiting on that special guy to call and afraid to leave the house in case he does."

"Pardon?"

Her mother shook her head. "Before cell phones, girls used to stay home staring at the phone hoping the guy they liked would call."

"That sounds lame and desperate."

Her mother cleared her throat.

"I'm not lame and desperate!" Even though the response burst out of her, Della's mind kept working. Hadn't the bakery been her entire life this past year? There were moments she was grateful for not having a pet because it would have taken time from her dream. Della blew out a long breath. "So, you think staying open past six is me waiting by the phone?"

"Exactly." Her mother pecked at her with an upraised finger as if pressing a button. "I'll tell you what my parents told me when I mooned around the house waiting for my high school crush to call me."

"Dad?" Della automatically assumed it was her father since her mother had never mentioned any other men in her life.

"Not your father." Mabel's eyes rolled upward and then dropped. "Good Heavens, I can't even remember his name now, which shows how unimportant he was. Anyhow, your grandmother told me to get out, do stuff, be seen having fun, and if he did call, I wouldn't be home, which would make me even more desirable. I would not be the needy girl by the phone who would be there whenever he called but instead the busy woman who didn't have time to wait around. You offer a great bakery with delicious food, but with definite hours. It would also allow you not to disappoint people who come by at seven looking for something we sold out of by two."

Her mother did have a valid point, and closing the shop early sounded entirely doable and reasonable. It also sounded easy, which was the opposite of working hard. "I don't know."

"I could have stayed home by the phone, wasting my time on a guy who never called. By the way, I met your father when I was out having fun. Who knows? You could be out enjoying yourself and meet potential customers in different places. Take some business cards with you. Don't be the needy bakery."

Since she didn't hide too much from her mother, she had to know about the delicate financial thin ice the bakery rested upon. "I am the needy bakery."

"Maybe so, but don't act like it. Fake it until you make it. If you don't shorten your hours, you'll burn out. Consider if you were paying an employee eleven dollars an hour to keep the place open. You'd be roughly paying the employee around three hundred dollars for hours worked. Add in the electricity, rent, and heat. Are you making so much money that it justifies the two of us being here?"

The valid point demonstrated her mother had thought out her argument and possibly rehearsed it. "It seems counterproductive to close early. However, I get your point. I'll make a sign to put up immediately. We'll have to mention it to every customer since people often don't read signs posted for their benefit."

"I'll make a point to mention it twice. What else do you have on your plate today?" Mabel asked as she made her way to the fridge, confident she'd made her point.

"Work here. Work at Lawson Industries. Maybe a look-see at Lawson's house on my lunch break. More work. Come by to close-up the bakery. Movie with Jaime. We might get a bite to eat afterward."

Her mother's walk toward the fridge stopped a foot before she reached her location and she spun around. "What's this about a look-see?"

"Oh, you know. Lawson is missing. I figured if his car were gone, there could be foul play involved."

"Foul play?" Her mother repeated the words and shook her head. "I was okay with the idea of Lawson getting cold feet and you talking him into going through with the wedding or at least alerting him he'd lose his deposit. If something has happened, the police should be on it. Besides, if Ethan didn't turn up anything, what makes you think you can?"

One gloved hand found purchase on her hip. "I'm not even sure Ethan tried that hard. He never showed up at Lawson Industries and questioned anyone. Wouldn't that be the first place to start?"

"Makes sense," her mother conceded and narrowed her eyes. "How would you know he didn't question anyone?"

"Puh-lease. I've been there less than a week, and I already know more about my fellow employees than I'm comfortable with. As far as gossip goes, some of them must have trained with Clarice. Besides, Kyle told me there had been a break-in at the building. Wouldn't he have mentioned a private investigator questioning everyone?"

"Good point." Her mother made the final step to the fridge to obtain the pre-mixed coffee makings. "So, how are things going with you and Kyle?"

It was just like her mother to pick up on that after everything she said. "Things *aren't* going. As you pointed out, I have no time since I'm in the bakery after hours. We talk. I guess I'd consider us acquaintances, maybe friends in the most casual manner."

"Oh."

Her mother's tone went down, suggesting disappointment. Sometimes, she felt like she was in one of those Regency romance novels where the main character's purpose in the story was to snag a husband. While her mother probably didn't consider it her daughter's main purpose in life, she *did* have a vested interest in making it happen.

"It'll be a quick look. If anyone sees me, I'll say I'm looking for property in the area and heard the place might be for sale. Sounds reasonable with the man getting married. He'd abandoned his bachelor digs for a home chosen with his fiancée." Della shrugged her shoulders. "Besides, what could possibly go wrong?"

CHAPTER NINETEEN

THE CUSTOMER SERVICE clock made its usual loud clicking sounds as the hands slowly inched toward noon. Della had brought in the promised sweets and a jar with black paper taped around it with *sweet treats $3* written in silver ink. Her mother came up with the idea of black paper, hoping to dissuade anyone who might be tempted by the sight of money in the jar. Tyesha suggested the box should be near her open door, and she'd keep an eye on the sweets and money. While most of the time her boss joked with the other employees—she kept a congenial attitude—most treated her with the respect one might accord a pit-bull.

Toby came in for lunch orders, and Della made a point of deferring, mentioning she had a few errands to run on her lunch hour. What she hadn't expected was a full inquiry from Lori and Jaime of what she had planned during lunch. Fortunately, the women didn't know her tells, so she stuck as close to the truth as possible, saying there was a house she wanted to look at, giving the impression she might be tired of apartment living. The last part was true.

Even though they called it lunch *hour*, it was only thirty minutes. Della dashed through the corridors to reach the elevator. Thank goodness she'd already programed the address into her GPS. To further her aim of a fast getaway, she had backed her car into a parking space, which was no easy thing since she didn't have a backup camera or skills when it came to reversing. With all this planning, she forgot to bring a lunch, which she remembered when her stomach prompted her with a growl. There was no time to eat because she had to hurry. Maybe there would be few pastries left in the box when she returned. It wasn't exactly the breakfast or lunch of champions, but it would have to do.

The modulated tones of the GPS directed her to make a sharp right turn. Thankfully, Della's low speed allowed her to do so without a hard slam to the brakes. Tall, graceful oaks and maple trees edged the street. Some had shed their leaves while others held onto their colorful garb. In the shadow of the trees stood modest brick ranch homes with single car garages. These types of neighborhoods used to be called the *factory* neighborhoods since they had sprung up when the auto manufacturing came to the area, bringing with it a slew of workers. The manufacturing jobs moved on, but some of the retired workers remained in neighborhoods such as this one.

Della checked her phone to see if she was in the right place. A red dot indicated the house was to her left. The orange brick home resembled those on either side of it, except for the color of the shutters and the unkempt yard. By the looks of it, Lawson didn't employ a lawn service. If the lawn didn't confirm it, the mailbox with pressed on numbers, and the name *Lawson* above it did. It wasn't fancy, but maybe the software industry wasn't as profitable as she thought it was. It fit into the profile of a practical man who refused to update his phones and clocks when they still worked.

Della chose not to park in the driveway but instead, parked on the street. All she had to do was peek inside the garage that fortunately had a window on the far side. With all the Ring cameras installed to prevent parcel thieves who often followed a delivery truck to steal what was left on a doorstep, Della needed to look both harmless and official. A clipboard that still had a catering checklist on it would serve. With it tucked under her arm, she exited her car.

She would be in and out in under five minutes and possibly have time to stop by a drive-thru on her way back. She walked by the mailbox, pretended to stumble, knocked into it, and dislodged the door as she straightened. Inside the opening lay a few pieces of junk mail. Della recognized a political flyer but couldn't say what the other item was. Judging by her own unending supply of advertisements and catalogs, a man who had been gone over a week should have more mail. Then again, maybe Lawson junior was smart enough to avoid mailing lists or had his mail sent to work. He could have also stopped his mail. As a remote possibility, he could even be at home. If it was the latter, Ethan had to be the worst private investigator around.

Della sidled up to the side of the garage, making a point to stare at her clipboard as if checking something out. She'd heard parcel thieves often carried a sack up to a front door, pretending to be food delivery.

An odd tickle started on her neck. The type of sensation people got when someone was staring at them. Since she didn't have a bag and there was no parcel on the porch, no one should worry about the old switcheroo. A neighbor could be keeping an eye on her, or Lawson could be in the house observing her every move.

With no time to overthink it, Della reached the high window, which forced her to rock up on her toes—still too high for her to see inside. Obviously, the builders wanted to let in light, but not allow any yahoo who happened to be moseying through the neighborhood to do any window shopping.

A quick inspection of possible assistance to reach the window revealed a folding lawn chair and a fluorescent orange, two foot tall, recycling bin. Imagining a twisted ankle or worse in her attempt to stand on it, she rejected the chair. The recycling bin turned upside down would serve the purpose.

Della carefully shook out a couple of tin cans and a 2-liter soda bottle, flipped over the bin, and situated it under the window. Using the wall to balance, she climbed up on it to peer inside the dim interior. Rather than a clear, lighted image, she saw shadows serving as silhouettes as for what could be inside. A long one had the shape and size of a car. If the car was here, where was its owner?

"What are you doing?"

The unexpected inquiry had Della stumbling back in surprise. Her fall ended as soon as it started as two masculine hands caught her and kept her upright. "Ah, thanks." She turned to face her rescuer and questioner. Kyle?

He kept his lips straight, but his eyes laughed at her. Della felt she should ask the obvious. "What are *you* doing here?"

Once she stood flat-footed on her own, Kyle dropped his hands and said, "I asked you first."

His lips finally gave in to the smile he was trying to suppress. "After all, you were the one looking in the window. I guess that makes you a peeping Jane. Maybe I should say a peeping Della." He chuckled at this as if it were the funniest thing he had heard in years.

"I suppose it does." She stalled, trying to remember what she'd said when first caught near Lawson's office. "I'm looking for Lawson, of course. His bride to be is making some outlandish and expensive requests. It only seems right to run it by him since he's footing the bill."

"Hmm…" Kyle gave a non-reply and crossed his arms. "You might not know this, but gossip makes the rounds in Owens. Bridezilla attempted to intimidate my Aunt Jessica, who owns The Cakery. Normally, my aunt is a kind, sweet woman, but she can only be pushed so far. Aunt Jessica dropped Bridezilla after she asked for a life-sized rendition of herself in cake form. Told her she wouldn't do it, and she refused to put up with her attitude one minute more."

Aunt Jessica sounded like someone Della should take lessons from. A door slammed and a woman exited from next door. Leaning on a cane, she moved in a direct diagonal to where Kyle and Della stood.

"You there!" the elderly woman called out. "You better not be up to no good. I have mace, and my nephew is on the police force. Clint Jackson. He's on speed dial."

Kyle waved to the woman. "I know Clint. He promised to put in a good word for me. I'm trying to get into the academy." Kyle wrapped an arm around Della as he continued speaking. "I heard this house might be up for sale. My cousin is a realtor, and I hoped to get a jump on everyone else. My soon-to-be bride and I are looking for a quiet place like this."

The elderly woman gave them both a thorough once over before speaking. "It's a good neighborhood. You could do worse. I didn't know Mr. Lawson was planning on selling, but I should have suspected as much. The soon-to-be missus has been over once or twice and acts too high in the instep to be content here."

An accurate assessment to be sure, Della thought, as she held her smile and bent slightly to retrieve her clipboard. She made sure to make eye contact with Kyle. "Gotta get back to work, sweetheart.

You're right, the house is perfect. Let me know when your cousin can show it."

She wiggled her fingers in the direction of the neighbor. "Nice meeting you."

As she walked in the direction of her car, she could hear Kyle and the neighbor talking. He even answered her inquiry about where he worked with a concise "Lawson Industries."

Hadn't anyone told him the more you say the more rope you give someone to hang you? The digital display on her car clock showed she had no time to wait for Kyle to discover his reasons for being at the house. A careful use of less busy secondary streets allowed her to return to work only five minutes late. An empty goodies box failed as her alternative plan for lunch.

While the vending machines might provide a salty and crunchy lunch in the form of chips, the phones were all ringing, and she was already late to her cubicle. Della slid into her chair and put on her headphones. About twenty minutes later, the calls slowed down and eventually stopped, giving the three women time to take off their headphones and scoot closer to chat.

Lori cleared her throat. "Well, look at that. I wonder who's getting flowers."

Both Jaime and Della turned to see what piqued their co-worker's interest. A smiling Kyle headed their way with a bundle of yellow roses and an aromatic bag from Senor Taco. Della desperately prayed the bag was for her or at least for someone who would share with her.

Lori called out in a sing-song voice. "Hello, Kyle! What has you in here so early *and* bearing flowers?"

"I thought I'd visit a friend and bring her lunch."

Lori pressed her hands over her heart. "For me? How sweet. Hate to tell you I already ate, but I could force myself to eat a taco. Jaime might take the roses."

Kyle shook his head and smiled. "Not today. I happen to know Della didn't have time to eat since I probably delayed her. The least I could do was bring her lunch."

No reason for her to look. Both Jaime and Lori would be throwing her speculative glances. Lori coughed, stood, and announced, "I need to get something to drink."

Jaime joined her and the two strolled toward the vending area. This would be the usual time for all phones to ring at once. However, the phones remained thankfully silent.

Della graciously accepted the tacos. "I'll pay you back for this."

"No need. Take the roses, too. It will brighten up your work area. Besides, you might consider them a form of peace offering."

This didn't sound good. She unwrapped a taco and was about to bite into it when she asked, "Why do you need a peace offering?"

The man sighed and looked off in the direction her co-workers took. "Not sure how long they will be gone. Gossip runs this town like gasoline powers cars. I know Ellie fired you from catering her wedding. I also know no one is willing to take your place in this town or the next. Everyone has her number. I doubt you were at the house to inform Lawson about Bridezilla's latest demand. More likely, you were there because you know something is up. That's why I was there. You may have heard senior Lawson is on his way. It seems fitting, as security, that I should at least have a clue what happened to his son."

"Okay." She bit into her taco, enjoying the spicy meat and crunchy tortilla. Personally, she hadn't heard too much that would upset her. "Why do you need a peace offering again?"

"Oh, that." Kyle chuckled. "I'm sure you'll be amused. I told you about my aunt. Apparently, when I told Lawson's neighbor my name, she turned out to be a friend of my aunt."

"That's nice." Della enjoyed another bite of the yummy taco and contemplated for a brief second pushing the rest of it into her mouth, but her mother taught her better manners than that. She glanced up at Kyle to see if he had finished speaking. His furrowed brow and pinched expression indicated concern. It had to be Lawson. "Find anything out about Lawson?"

"No." He gave hearty sigh. "I was hoping you might know something."

Her mind drifted back to the strange knocking at Stephanie's house, being run off the road, and the very confusing Ethan Stone and his peculiar work habits. "I'm not sure. Some odd things *have* happened lately."

"Good." Kyle rubbed his hands together. "We should get together and talk about this. Oh, I should tell you my aunt now thinks you and I are engaged. Gotta go. I'll call you later."

The taco bite she just took stuck in her throat. Della watched silently as Kyle sprinted down the corridor.

CHAPTER TWENTY

WHEN YOUR MOTHER has spent a good part of her life helping you, the polite thing is to listen to her advice. It doesn't mean you have to agree with it or even follow it. With any luck, she might distract her mother by introducing a different subject. Della used a melon baller to scoop the fragrant lemon drop cookie dough into perfect spheres onto the parchment-lined cookie sheet. She'd occasionally look up at her mother and make a non-committal noise to prove her attentiveness.

"You know, business has picked up since last month. People are buying entire boxes of cookies to take to work. I think we should sign on with those delivery services that zoom all around town with people's food orders."

"Sounds good," Della agreed, but added, "They charge a high premium for that service. Lots of local restaurants have already dropped them because it was too expensive."

"What about mailing cookies? With the right packaging, we could get them there fresh and unbroken. Great for college students away from home." Mabel wiggled her eyebrows, possibly aware there wasn't much of a downside to her suggestion.

"Doable."

It sounded like her mother had given the matter some thought but she hadn't brought down the hammer yet. She would. Della had made the mistake of telling her about Kyle and her teaming up with him to find the missing heir.

"We got two orders for birthday cakes yesterday. One of them was an employee from Lawson Industries."

"Mom…" She kept her voice even in an effort not to sound whiny. After all, she was almost thirty, not thirteen. "Those all are good things, but it's petty cash. Let's say the wedding is off. It feels that way to me. Let's focus on Lawson Industries, the town's major employer, and the fact that customer dissatisfaction with the accompanying bad public relations is killing the company image. Jeffrey Lawson needs to be found to deal with this. He could be hurt. Someone needs to rescue him."

Mabel picked up a spatula and used it as an extension of her arm, pointing it in her daughter's direction. "That's why you need to stay out of it. Let the police handle it."

Why did she have to open her big mouth? It just felt ironic that Kyle was trying to track down Lawson, too. Apparently, Mom missed the irony of the situation. A wave of heat blew into her face as she opened the doors of the convection oven and slid in the finished cookie sheet.

"The police won't do anything because he's an adult, and there's no ransom, and no sign of foul play. They will assume, like most people have, that the man is hiding from his very own bridezilla, hoping she'll take the hint and vanish."

"Well…" Her mother hesitated and reached back to rub her neck with her free hand. "That might have been true before, but once senior hits town, stuff will get done. As you pointed out, Lawson is the biggest employer in town, which makes him an important guy. As he's a blood relative, the police would have to take his missing person report seriously."

"Barbie, his assistant, filed one on day two of his absence."

The spatula hit the counter with a slap as her mother gaped at her for a second. "You're just telling me this now?"

"I didn't know. Kyle informed me. Security personnel know more than the regular workers, especially a temp. Barbie was told they'd investigate it, but if Lawson Junior was safe, they didn't have to tell her where he was. After all, he's an adult."

"You're right." She bobbed her head and picked up the spatula again to use it on the cooling espresso chocolate crinkles. Her voice dropped a little as she continued. "He's not acting much like an adult, though. I'm not sure what you and Kyle think you can do. Ethan didn't turn up anything. Did Ellie report him missing?"

That was an excellent point. The thought had crossed her mind, especially after the woman tried to change the menu. "No. Kyle has some friends on the force. They must feed him information, but none of them said anything about Ellie filing a report. It could be she knows where he is. They could be talking on a regular basis, or she doesn't care overly much as long as he shows up for the wedding and foots the bills. She plans on having the wedding of the century come Hell or high water."

Her mother snorted and grumbled too low for Della to hear as she moved cooled cookies onto the tray for the display case.

"What?"

"I said..." She spoke louder and with emphasis. "...if your father were missing, I wouldn't be flitting around trying to change up wedding plans. I'd be on the phone every day calling the police, and I'd be doing my own legwork, trying to see where he was last." She cut her eyes to Della. "I guess that's what *you're* doing."

"In a way." She didn't want her mother to be worried. "Besides, I'll be with Kyle, and he's licensed to carry a gun."

"Just stop, now!" Her mother shook her head hard and pressed her free hand to her heart. "My mental images of you sneaking around just turned into a firefight."

Time to change the subject. Della hefted an oversized bowl of chocolate chip dough onto the counter. The time-honored cookie sold out almost every day. "How's Horace? How did the second date go?"

"It was okay. We went to Ginger's Café. I ordered the special, which was beef stroganoff. The meat was very tender."

Her mother smiled briefly, picked up the tray and carried it into the other room. That was it? After encouraging her mother for seven years to go out on a date, the summary of the restaurant special was all Della got. Yesterday, Mabel found the middle-aged man pouting when he lost at miniature golf charming.

Della trailed her mother into the café area. "What's wrong?"

Instead of answering, Mabel opened the case and slid in the tray of cookies. She turned to face her daughter and grimaced. "I should have known better. He isn't your father."

"That's to be expected. I only had one father and wouldn't expect anyone else to be like him. Keep in mind, this man isn't necessarily the love of your life. You're meeting for conversation and to see if there could be a spark between you."

Her response sounded a great deal like something her mother would say when she tried to fix Della up with someone's single or a newly divorced son who couldn't manage to secure a date on his own.

"I know." Her mother sighed as she walked back into the kitchen with Della trailing her. "You may not remember that I was a good friend of Eileen's, Horace's ex-wife. Even though it's been twenty-plus years since she left, I do remember some of the things she said. I'd kind of forgotten them until the dinner date. With the miniature golf, we were moving around and chasing after balls. With the dinner date, I was stuck at the table and served as a captive audience as Horace waxed on about his favorite subject–Horace."

Some people didn't make good initial impressions, but her mother knew Horace longer than she knew Della, so that excuse wouldn't work. "Did he talk about anything else?"

"Headlights."

Was this supposed to be code for something? "Excuse me?"

"You know, the lights for your car. He collects them. Suddenly, I remember Eileen claiming his headlight collection grew like mushrooms in the dark. A stream of light would cause one to reflect, looking all the world like an eye staring at you in the middle of the night. Eerie. I imagine he's had plenty of time to collect more in the last twenty years. I declined when he asked for another date. I told him the bakery kept me busy."

"You'll need a better excuse than that. He'll start hanging out here." A lovelorn mechanic waiting for a glimpse of her mother, she didn't need.

"Working on it. Back in the day, I could say I was going back with my old boyfriend. That seemed to work well enough." Mabel held up one finger with a smile. "I got it. Your father to the rescue, once again. I'm just not ready to date yet."

It might be true. More likely, she wasn't ready to date Horace now and wouldn't be ready anytime in the future. Headlights? People collected different objects, but headlights weren't exactly tiny or would fit into a display album. There was a good chance the house resembled more of a salvage yard. "No worries. Don't expect a love connection on your first date."

Mabel placed one hand on her hip and pursed her lips before speaking. "Please tell me you aren't using the same phrases I use on you to encourage you to date more."

"Could be," she admitted with a smirk as she filled another cookie sheet. "How does it feel to be on the other end?"

"Ha! You're the funny one now. So, what are you and Kyle planning to do in your combined investigation?"

There was no need to tell her mother they planned to nose around Stephanie's house to see if she might be hiding Lawson in the basement. "It's better if you don't know just in case things go south."

The flat of her mother's hand went up in Della's direction, signaling her to cease speaking. "Another thing I could do without knowing."

CHAPTER TWENTY-ONE

THE PEPPY MORNING deejay rattled on about another glorious autumn day as Della drove. Back when she was in high school, she imagined being an adult would be this glorious thing with tons of leisure time to do things she'd never done in high school, such as speeding around the racetrack in a Formula One car or jumping out of an airplane. Her nose crinkled at the last two mental images since she hadn't wanted to do either. That was from a commercial about how your life would change when your credit score went up— another thing she didn't need to dwell on.

She eased her foot off the gas and transferred it to the brake as the light changed. As a careful driver, Della usually kept her attention on the light, making sure she could move forward promptly and avoid having the person behind her honk, who, if they had planned their day better, wouldn't have had to rush around. So far, she'd had very few honks in her life, both those of the irritated sort and the provocative type to approve of a woman walking down the street.

Once, when she and Celeste, her high school buddy, were crossing the street in front of the library, a car honked. For a sheer second, Della inhaled deeply, thinking, at last, some guy approved of what he saw even though it was a chauvinist reaction. Turned out, it was Layne, her other best friend, in the car. Thank goodness she never admitted to anyone she had taken secret delight thinking she'd been honk worthy. However, now, as an adult female, she'd want nothing to do with someone who resorted to honking as opposed to a friendly wave.

The light lasted longer than usual. Her eyes cut over to the car in the turn lane, gauging if the driver felt the same. The man stared straight ahead with the same chiseled profile as Ethan, and the same well-trimmed beard. His right hand, with the same ornate school ring on the ring finger as Ethan, held a cup up to his lips. Ethan Stone never left town! Her teeth ground together. The man lied to her. Pieces of the puzzle started to come together.

A loud honk interrupted her puzzle-solving, causing a knee-jerk reaction to floor the car when Ethan turned. Where was the man going? Did he have a lead on Lawson's location? Maybe she should have followed him—not that it would do her any good, except make her late for her customer service job. When it came to information, Ethan might as well be nicknamed Scrooge. Besides, she and Kyle might crack the case wide open today.

At some point, she might mention her bakery, and Lawson would be so grateful that he'd vow to use it forever and tell his friends to do so, too. Knowing what she did about Ellie, she couldn't bring herself to urge the man to go through with the wedding, even if he might be willing just to have a high maintenance chick by his side.

Her mental musings ground to a halt when logic made an appearance. Ha! It wasn't like the two of them would break out a basement window and pull a weakened software heir through it.

Despite sticking points such as not being an action hero or knowing where the man was, other scenarios took form with a grateful Lawson thanked her for her diligence.

The perky deejay fielded calls about what was right in people's lives. The format allowed people to announce events such as birthdays, anniversaries, or new jobs. Normally, the excited voices cheered her as someone gushed about their darling child or thoughtful husband. Today, it grated on her nerves. Her hand hovered over the power button when a gravelly voice sounded. "I saw something yesterday that has me worried. You should be worried, too."

Her hand fell away, even though she suspected it would be a segue for a product. Perky Deejay asked the caller to continue.

"My brother-in-law has one of those small planes. He thinks it makes him a big shot and all." The man sniffed before continuing. "I agreed to go up with him, hoping it would be a way to stop him from asking."

Perky Deejay cut in. "Good for you. I imagine most of our listeners would have enjoyed being in your place."

"I'm not finished."

"Go on. Make it short because we have news at the top of the hour."

"This *is* news. I saw an entire line of black SUVs heading toward Owens. They were taking the back roads, too, possibly not wanting to be seen."

The deejay chuckled. "I guess we have a visiting dignitary in the area. Thanks for calling."

"Wait."

Curiosity built as Della contemplated a slew of dark SUVs heading their way. Owens wasn't where the jet-set headed for a good time. With any luck, the caller would make his point before she entered the subterranean parking garage and lost her signal.

"Aliens. They're here. It's a—" A different voice cut in and asked who to call when you needed a plumber, with a jingle complete with the phone number. The deejay had allowed the caller to say his piece longer than most. Aliens. Why did it always come back to that? The caller might as well have said the Queen of England was visiting.

The incident forgotten, Della parked and exited the car, juggling her large box of treats. A good three hours of apologizing to irate callers before connecting them to the Tech Department, who wouldn't bother to answer, awaited her. Why should they when they knew nothing about the product and, in turn, couldn't advise the angry caller? It made no sense why Lawson Industries would make a wide left turn into a photo enhancement software when they'd never done such a thing before.

It *had* provided her with a job, but it wouldn't last forever. There were only so many people who would buy the software. From what little she'd heard from her callers, it was difficult to use, and made the user insert the tweaked photo directly into dating profiles, resume loaders, or social media from the software.

A few had been content with their image and wanted to use it for actual photos or as their Christmas card photo, but that hadn't worked. It didn't make much sense to her because she'd easily loaded tweaked photos, even the one where it looked like she was swimming with polar bears, onto the photo book site. Nothing made sense about the Glamorize software and why the company was still promoting it.

Co-workers greeted her as she made her way to her work station. A few even trailed her, waiting for her to set down the box and set up her money jar. Della usually vacated the break room area where she left the goodies after she placed a stack of napkins and business cards beside the box. She preferred to think the pastries would sell themselves. Besides, she needed to get a head start on work. She couldn't be sure extracting the younger Lawson wouldn't take longer than her lunch hour. It all depended on whether an upset Stephanie was detaining the man. A fat envelope filled with mainly ones and fives, a couple of tens, and a twenty were zippered into the front pocket of her purse.

If Stephanie were home, Della would go up to the front door after Kyle worked his way around the house to the basement windows. She'd distract the woman by talking about the refund or something. Somehow, she'd have to stretch out the story to give Kyle the needed time. As plans went, it wouldn't be used in any upcoming movies. If they did confirm Jeffrey Lawson was being held against his will, they'd simply call the police while keeping an eye on the house just in case the kidnapper might try to move him.

Phones kept ringing despite the three of them handling calls. It sure didn't sound like sales were drying up. Della shifted in her seat and arched her back to get more comfortable. The upcoming sleuthing session created knots in her stomach, and sweaty palms. Just thinking about what might happen made her a little nauseated. This wasn't what she wanted, sneaking around, handing off envelopes of money she could ill afford, all while trying to keep her bakery afloat.

Underneath the constant strident ringing of the phones, a gentle burble of her own cell had Della reaching for her purse. Kyle messaged her his location as in the garage and waiting for her.

SHE FINISHED UP her client call and stood up. "Gotta run some errands during lunch."

Her co-workers nodded in her direction and smirked at each other. Lori glanced at the roses Kyle had brought before adding, "Enjoy your *lunch*."

"Yeah," she added, aware her fellow employees thought she would be enjoying a romantic lunch as opposed to snooping around. "I'll be back as soon as I can."

The office door opened, and Tyesha stepped out with a grin. "I guess I should point out the walls are like paper. I can hear everything you say. Take your time, Della. One of us should be having fun. We'll want details." She crinkled her nose, giggled, and gestured for her to leave. "Get out of here."

Della grabbed her purse and walked until she got to the corridor where she broke into a slow jog. It would convince any observers that she couldn't wait for her lunch date. Normally, she'd take the elevator, but it wasn't all that fast and probably full of people who'd chatter incessantly. Apparently, no one told them you didn't talk in the elevator. Stairs, it was. By the time she reached Kyle, her heart pounded and not from fear.

The GPS on her phone issued directions to Stephanie's house. Both Kyle and Della spoke little, each possibly lost in their own thoughts. A flash of light in a side-view mirror drew her focus as opposed to continuing to dwell on what could possibly go wrong. Was that Ethan behind them? Della unlatched her seatbelt and twisted in her seat to check out her initial assumption. The car immediately turned right without signaling or even slowing down. Suspicious, or possibly just a bad driver—it was hard to know.

The brick entry sign announcing the neighborhood, along with the GPS's assertion to turn now, had Kyle doing so. Not much had changed since her last visit. One resident carried colorful mums from her car while another walked an elderly poodle. Many of the residents were retired factory workers, which meant they had plenty of time to be home unlike folks who spent eight to ten hours away from their home. It brought up the question of how would a woman smuggle a non-compliant Lawson into her house without attracting notice?

She wouldn't. More likely she had invited him inside. Another turn and Stephanie's house came into view. "It's on your left. Drive past it. Park in front of the house with the metal sunflowers."

Kyle followed her instructions without any comment. Almost anyone else she knew would either argue with her or do it their way.

After switching off the engine, Kyle sighed. "I wish I'd had a chance to check out the house beforehand, but I'll do the best I can."

"Me, too." Della held up one finger. "Remember, if anyone catches you in their yard, you're looking for our puppy, Tootsie Roll. She's a chocolate lab. The poor dear ran away when we stopped because she saw another puppy. I should have noticed her puppy restraint was chewed through."

"Ah…" Kyle winked. "A good story makes the best alibi. Let's do this."

CHAPTER TWENTY-TWO

D ELLA DONNED A pair of sunglasses as she waited in the truck. A single ray broke through the clouds, saturating the vehicle in white light. It made her eyewear practical but kept her from viewing where Kyle was in his search-for-the-puppy process. Even though it had been her plan, she hadn't given it too much thought—such as bringing a leash. The detachable shoulder strap on her purse served if no one looked at it too closely.

All the man needed was a couple of minutes to get into the back yard before Della started her approach. It might have been better if she had Stephanie's number and called to keep her from peering into her back yard. Why the woman would try to carry out such a nefarious plan?

A mail carrier walked by with a full bag and nodded in the truck's direction. A person didn't go unnoticed in this neighborhood, especially a stranger acting peculiar. If they didn't hurry, the police would be called on them. Still, nothing had happened to Stephanie. It could be like all those news reports after a serial killer has been arrested, with the neighbors commenting on what a nice, polite man he was.

A quick glance at her phone showed it was time for her to act. Inhaling deeply, she depressed the truck handle and slid out of the oversized truck. She walked quickly while mentally reassuring herself. Technically, she wasn't doing anything wrong. Hadn't she told Stephanie she would give the money back and here she was with the money? Kyle wasn't planning to break into the house, just peek into the window for evidence. A tied up and gagged Jeffrey Lawson would serve the purpose, but an open cot might be enough for police to investigate. Still, many people had cots, and some stored them in the basement, which wasn't exactly what the LEOs would consider proof.

A car door slammed in the distance, but Della didn't bother to look since that's what a guilty person who was up to no good might do. She reached the front door and noticed only the glass security door stood closed, allowing Della a glimpse into the house. Two suitcases stood close to the door, indicating a fast getaway in the upcoming minutes. Warning lights went off in Della's head. The only thing between Stephanie and her car was Della. Her top teeth sank into her lip as she debated what to do.

Most television private investigators relied on guile and faked good nature to put the suspect at ease as opposed to tackling them. A few had a gun, which she didn't. Her handbag held a variety of strange objects, but most had to do with catering. Della shook her purse and slipped her hand in, hoping for something pointy and pulled out a food thermometer. It *did* have a dull point but would not strike fear into anyone.

She dropped the thermometer back into her purse, and tried again for something that could be used as a weapon when she heard a woman shout, "Jethro! Jethro. Come here right now!"

She had an accomplice! Her muscles tensed, and she pulled out a corkscrew. Not going to work either—she needed to abort, but also needed to let Kyle know before he got hurt. A huge dog raced into the living room, skidded to a stop, taking one of the area rugs with it, and barked when it saw Della.

A frazzled Stephanie raced into the room, grabbing the big dog's collar, and acting unaware of the lurker at her front door. The dog barked again and tried to surge toward the front door, forcing the woman to look.

"Oh! I didn't see you there. Did you knock?"

Della hadn't, but to admit to standing there would be odd. "A little," Della said with a strained smile. "I guess you didn't hear me."

"Yeah, you're right." She glanced down at the dog she was restraining. The oversized creature could be part mastiff, some Great Dane, and a few other dogs thrown in. "I was trying to wrangle Jethro into the car. We're going on a trip."

Most criminals wouldn't admit their plans unless they were very cool cucumbers or creating a fake alibi. "Oh! How nice for you two."

"Not really," Stephanie admitted and fondled the big dog's ears. "My mother isn't doing too well, and there isn't anyone else to help out. I figure it's the right thing to do. The only problem is Jethro hates to travel. It's probably because he usually ends up at the vet whenever he gets in the car."

While Della liked dogs, she didn't consider herself an expert on handling them. Right now, her analytical brain juggled the idea of a caring daughter against a possible kidnapper. What if the kidnapping had been an impulsive act? Her brow furrowed as she considered kidnapping against a random purchase such as boots that she didn't need but were cute and on clearance. Boots were understandable, but not so with kidnapping, especially when the victim would resist. Boots never resisted. Surely Kyle had done what he needed to do by now. All she needed to do was hand over the money.

"I'm glad I caught you before you headed out. Where does your mother live?"

"Tucson. In one of those villages for older folks with names that make them sound much nicer than they are. Hers is called Pine Woods, although there isn't a pine tree in sight. So, why are you here?"

"Your refund." Della discreetly dropped the corkscrew in the purse and removed the bulging money envelope. The possibility of the woman being a kidnapper melted away with every word she spoke. If she wasn't, they had nothing.

"Oh." Stephanie shrugged her shoulders and pulled on her dog's collar, moving him backward. "Let me put up Jethro. I can't take a chance on his escaping. It would take me forever to catch him. The dog loves to run."

The sound of dog claws against linoleum helped her know the dog's current location as they disappeared. Then she heard a screen door open and close. Della's heart skipped a beat. The back yard! She hoped Kyle had gotten in and left by now. She rotated in a slow circle, trying to catch sight of Kyle. No luck—overgrown hedges blocked any easy ganders over the fence. Currently, Della couldn't even spot the fence as she backed up a few steps. Now would be the perfect time to leave, except she hadn't given Stephanie the money. Maybe she could open the door, throw the money in, and hightail it out of here. Surely Kyle had made it back to the truck.

A human yelp followed by barking answered that question. Her partner in subterfuge raced around the corner of the house with Jethro in pursuit. Kyle must not have shut the gate as he fled the yard.

Della dropped her purse, spilling the money envelope and ran into the yard just as Jethro knocked Kyle down and sunk his teeth into the leather jacket. She rushed to Kyle but slid to a stop, not knowing how to disengage the pooch who happily munched on the jacket and possibly Kyle.

A car door slammed, followed by running feet. Ethan appeared, along with another unknown man, as Stephanie sprinted out of the house, grabbed Jethro's collar, and hauled the dog off its latest chew toy.

Thank goodness for small favors. Della had no clue how to handle the oversized canine. Relieved the burden of saving Kyle didn't rest on her, she focused on the second complication. "Ethan! What are you doing here?"

For a man who had left town, he sure was around a lot.

The noise brought several neighbors to their front stoops. Stephanie waved them away. "Just Jethro! Everything is under control!"

About that time, an errant breeze blew some bills across the lawn—the money she'd worked so hard to get.

"The money!" Della scampered after it, grabbing bills. Both Kyle and the unknown man helped her. Finally, they rounded up the money, and Ethan motioned them into the house with a tight-lipped look.

Her footsteps slowed as she approached the house. She cut her eyes to Kyle. Did he have a clue what was happening or misgivings about entering the house? Ethan hadn't told her the whole truth, that much she knew. Why was he here and wanted them all in the house?

Della made a point to scoop up her purse when a clammy chill came over her that had nothing to do with the weather. Maybe the meat thermometer and the corkscrew might be useful after all.

Once inside, she noticed no Jethro. "The dog?"

"In the basement."

A dull thud like the one Della heard previously came from the direction of the basement. "Someone's in the basement."

Stephanie shook her head. "That's Jethro. He uses his ropey toy to knock on the door. The first time he did it, he scared me to death. I almost didn't open the door, convinced there was someone on the other side."

Well, that explained that, although Della would have liked to have seen the dog making a knocking sound. It would have saved her from this present situation, whatever it was. "Ah, here's your money. A little wrinkled after chasing it across the yard. I hope I got it all."

Stephanie started to reach for the money, then pulled her hand back. "I can't take it. I'll admit I could use the money, especially for the trip. When you came by, I wasn't in the best of moods, what with trying to work out what I was going to do about my mother. I figured you were just talk and if I got some money, then good." She pressed her lips together and grimaced. "Mr. Lawson already came by and apologized for my trouble. He even gave me money from his own wallet. Then he asked me to keep calling and complaining and gave me numbers to say, such as 'this is my thirty-first call.'"

Ethan's head snapped up. "That's it. He was trying to send a message, but no one who knew the code was getting it. What else did he say? Anything?"

Stephanie played with the ends of her hair as her eyes rolled upward. "I appreciate the money. I thought it was weird of him to give it to me. He just took out his wallet and counted the bills out

THE WEDDING CAKE BLUES

and apologized for the trouble. I kept thinking it was strange for the boss of a company to come visit me. He said something about going to a cabin in the woods."

Ethan pulled out a cell and typed into it. Della had already visited Lawson's house, and she had seen the car in the garage. "What was he driving?"

Her question had Ethan raising his head and gained the attention of the unknown man.

Kyle, aware of what she was asking, blurted out, "His car was in his garage."

Ethan grumbled about going way beyond the efforts of an average caterer. The way he said it didn't make it sound like a good thing. It grated, mainly because she hadn't found Lawson. Nothing was turning out to be the slam dunk she thought it would be. "At least *I* didn't give up on the man, like you did."

A snort served as an answer. "I didn't give up. I fell back because you weren't giving me any information. You even took the job at Lawson that was supposed to be Delvin's." He gestured to the man beside him.

The dark, intense man would not have been a good fit in customer service. "Oh, he wouldn't have liked it."

"That was the plan, anyway. We told Lawson he could signal through the company and an agent would be in place, but then there wasn't, because of you. I think he even told them who to hire. I don't understand what went wrong."

Della's initial apprehension slipped away only to be replaced by confusion. "What's going on?"

Ethan reached into his jacket which resulted in Kyle lunging across the space separating the two and grabbing the man's hand.

They both tumbled to the ground, causing Jethro to break into frenzied barking on the other side of the door.

"Stop!" The command had them all looking at Delvin, who had assumed a firing stance and had his gun pointed at Kyle.

She hadn't even considered the unknown man a threat. Big mistake. Kyle held up his hands and slowly stood, shooting a questioning glance at Della. Nope, she was clueless and regretful. She had somehow gotten Kyle involved. Even though the man wasn't the love of her life, he did try to shield her when possible danger loomed.

Ethan frowned as he pushed off the floor, reached into his pocket, pulled out a wallet, and flipped it open to display a badge.

"This was what I was trying to do before being attacked. Delvin, no need for the gun. I think our friends will remain calm."

Friends? Della didn't recognize the badge and held her hand out for it. Even though not much happened of the felonious nature in Owens, the local law enforcement wouldn't take kindly to others horning in on their territory. Her father never did. Butting in where they didn't belong, causing trouble where there was none, and in general, getting in the way of solid police work were some of her father's favorite complaints against the FBI. Owens never really had much reason to attract the attentions of the Federal Bureau of Investigation. A newspaper article, some inner office chatter at the police station, or even a popular crime drama would send her dad into full rant mode.

She read the badge out loud. "Federal Bureau of Investigation. FBI. Why in the world would you be in a small town like Owens?"

Ethan shook his head and held his hand out for his badge. "Ah, you small-town types never have a clue what's happening right under your noses."

His condescending tone irritated. It made her wonder if his name was even Ethan. She flipped open the badge to check and noted it was Ethan, but not Stone. As names went, Ethan was common enough. She started to hand back the badge, but Stephanie put out her hand.

"I'd like to see it. I'm not sure how all this stuff started happening to me. Sure, I bought some software that wasn't that easy to use. It certainly didn't get me the dates I wanted when I uploaded my photo. After complaining a few times—maybe more than a few—Lawson shows up in that 1970s turquoise Jeep Chief." She held up one finger. "I remembered it because my mother's sister used to have a car like that. I remember thinking at the time it wasn't a color I'd expect a man to buy. It also made me wonder how profitable the software business was if he was driving a car older than I am."

Delvin glanced down at his phone and typed a few words. "Did you get the license plate?"

"Of course not. I had no clue I'd need it. Besides, how many cars that old would be registered in this state?" She stabbed her finger in Ethan's direction. "I'm not thrilled about your attitude or your partner waving a gun. This is my house, and I didn't invite you." She turned slightly to take in the full group. "I have no clue why you're here. I *do* know I need to get on the road soon."

The woman had gumption. Della liked how she didn't take any guff and had a quick mind. Very few people ever catch license numbers, and even when they think they do, they usually get the numbers wrong.

"I'd like to know, too." Emboldened by Stephanie's show of bravado, Della found her own courage and outrage. "You come into my bakery, pretend to flirt with me, all the while trying to find out what I know about Lawson."

Her statement didn't have the desired result. Instead, Kyle grumbled from his position. "You mean you're not her cousin?"

Ethan shook his head. "Nope. The field is wide open, pal."

His cavalier comment didn't appeal. It sounded like a woman had no say in romantic matters, but men battled it out like mountain goats. Della liked him better when he was pretending to be charming. It certainly explained the ups and downs of his personality. As far as she could tell, Ethan hadn't uncovered a thing.

Still, the man postured like a banty rooster. He pocketed his badge and placed his hands on his hips. "Tell you what. Keep your mouths shut and give me your contact numbers. We have work to do, but later, I'll have to debrief you all."

Debriefing? What would that involve?

CHAPTER TWENTY-THREE

T HE PARTITION WALLS that separated the different conference rooms on the ground level of the Lawson Industries building were folded back to accommodate the large crowd. Spicy scents drifted from the taco bar and mingled with the heavy sweetness wafting off the dessert table. Della carried a large tray of shrimp cocktails out to the buffet table, smiling a little as she did so. It might not be the tiger shrimp Ellie had demanded, which resulted in Della pursing her lips, knowing any type of shrimp cocktail wouldn't be on the prison menu.

A deejay spun dance tunes and invited the crowd to get up and boogie. Lori and Jaime took him up on the invite, often snagging other co-workers as they pranced to the dance floor.

The lanky figure of Jeffrey Lawson cut through the crowd. He stopped now and then to greet his employees and local dignitaries. He finally reached the buffet table where Della arranged the cocktails in concentric circles, aware they'd only be beautifully designed until the horde noticed them.

"Everything looks great," Lawson remarked and picked up an almond cookie, popped it into his mouth, and chewed. "They taste as good as they look. I'm glad you talked me into turning a failed wedding reception into a gratitude celebration for Lawson Industries."

"We'd already ordered the food." She could have saved it for another affair, but she decided to take a chance and suggested a party for the employees. New clocks and phones would be welcomed, but Della didn't know the company bottom line after the disastrous Glamorize roll out. She did know Lawson had a lot to clean up, which had kept him so busy they hadn't had time to really talk since the debriefing.

"It's good for the employees," she commented.

"So right. They deserve something after dealing with the fallout from Glamorize." He grabbed a plate and piled it high with meatballs, tiny quiches, and fruit skewers. "Hiding out in my father's old fishing cabin, waiting for the heat to die down, made me miss the little things like cell service, decent folks, and delicious food. I didn't know who to trust and hoped Ethan would get my messages. He was my handler."

The term had Della wrinkling her nose. "It makes you sound like you're at a dog show. Where is he anyway? I haven't seen him since the debriefing session, which was basically don't talk about it and if you do talk about it, we'll know, which felt somewhat threatening." The memory of the experience made her understand her father's disdain a little more.

Della pressed a hand against her chest. "I'm not even sure what I'm not supposed to talk about since I don't know much. If he means not mentioning how I crept around your place, peeking in windows, I'll keep that to myself, but I can't say the same for your neighbor."

He laughed. "I know which one you mean. Ethan doesn't have a handle on small towns. He commented that law enforcement was lacking, leaving it wide open for criminal activity, but I think we do all right."

Considering her father had been part of the thin blue line that kept the town safe, Della had similar sentiments. "We do. We're not like some of those burgs who are distribution drug rings. Despite all that, I bet Ethan is trading war stories with the other handlers about how he saved Owens and Lawson Industries."

"Possibly. Still, I must give him some credit. Initially, I didn't want to be involved but felt I had to save the company. If it ever came out, the scandal could ruin us. As it is, people get a refund, complain now and then, but consider the company a good sport since we righted a wrong."

He grimaced and bit a meatball off a colored toothpick. He chewed before continuing. "I needed a handler because I had no clue what to do. Ellie pushed me into accepting Glamorize, telling me I needed to move Lawson Industries into the twenty-first century. I had no clue it enabled spies to communicate via dating apps with no one being the wiser."

"All of that stuff still confuses me. I understand a little about them saying middleware ran in the background, starting on its own and running on its own without anyone being aware. Oh, and that even without it, spies could create a dating profile or change words in the profile to leave messages for other spies."

The few times Della pulled up dating profiles, she'd wondered it there might be a knack to translating them. Now she knew more than she wanted to. "So, in a profile, someone might say, 'must love dogs,' meaning something like, 'let's meet at our predetermined place?'"

"Maybe. Maybe a person saying they hate sushi could mean their cover is blown." Lawson cocked his head and peered off into the distance.

"The spies must have a complete list of what the codes mean. Perhaps they memorize them. As you've probably guessed, I wasn't told much more than they told all of us."

He shrugged his shoulders. "There had to have already been some rumors flying around before I got involved. No sooner did Glamorize appear on the market, than I was contacted and told not to tell anyone since they hoped to flush out the culprits."

The whole affair resembled a movie, especially the part about the mean, high maintenance chick being the villain. The image of being run off the road came back. "Do you think Ellie might have tried to run over me?"

Instead of answering, Lawson speared another meatball from his plate and chewed. Finally, he spoke. "Hard to say. She's a really bad driver. Hey, I didn't even suspect I was being played for the fool."

There was no reason to point out that men didn't always choose girlfriends based on their sterling character and good deeds. "Why should you suspect your fiancée was one of the bad guys? Any man would be overwhelmed by a beautiful woman like Ellie."

"I suppose." He shivered. "Scary to think how close I came to marrying her. I should have been suspicious from the get-go since Ellie had no interest in me until I took over the company. Suddenly, I was honey. Don't remember proposing, but I do remember her telling me when the wedding was, where it would be, and that I was paying."

"Do you think she would have gone far enough to have married you?" she asked, it being something she'd wondered about even before she knew about the woman's spying activities. It wasn't the most appropriate question, but rather more like something her mother might ask.

"I guess it depended on how long she needed me for her plan to work. We could have married, and then one day she'd have vanished to wherever spies go—maybe have some cosmetic work done and head for South America or someplace where they don't extradite wanted folks."

"Makes sense. I appreciate your filling me in more. Your friends in the black SUVs didn't. They came in and pushed me around for information. When that didn't work, they followed me around. At first, I thought I needed to find you to see if you'd just gotten cold feet. After Ellie hounded me about all her changes and then threatened me when I wouldn't give in, I just wanted to find you to tell you to run or stay hidden."

He gave a quick bob of acknowledgment as Mabel headed toward them, pushing a metal cart loaded with cookies. Her mother veered toward Della and hissed, "I have a big surprise for you."

After the last few days, she could live without anything unexpected happening. She forced a polite smile and muttered, "I think I'll pass."

"You'll love him. His name is Antonio." Her mother grinned and moved on to the cookie table.

Her mother should know how she felt about matchmaking. It wasn't as if she'd been reticent about previous attempts. Oh well, she'd deal with it later. It's not like Antonio was hiding in the kitchen, and she wanted to finish her conversation with Lawson to find out what exactly happened. Della straightened some serving plates as she worked her way closer to Lawson.

"I was wondering what happened with my being hired as opposed to Delvin."

Jeffrey smirked. "You've met Tyesha. I wrote something about hiring a temp. I was rushing around, not knowing who I could trust. I'm not sure if I wrote out Delvin's whole name. Tyesha could have also decided she didn't want a man in her department and ignored it anyway. Tried to make it right by sneaking into my office to access my own computer, and all I did was set off the alarm systems." He pulled a comical face. "So many alarm systems. Here I thought I'd disabled them all until I heard the buzzing. Got out before Kyle came charging upstairs, gun drawn, but never got out my message about Delvin. I was forced to hope for the best. In the end, it worked out. You might have not known what the numbers meant, but you never gave up."

She'd never answered a call from Stephanie, which meant Delvin could have been in the same situation. "You know, I never talked to Stephanie before I knocked on her door. You're just lucky I'm so nosy and persistent."

He gave her a hearty pat on the back that made Della grateful she wasn't holding anything.

"I wish I could pay you or something."

"You already have." Della gestured to the spread of food. "If you want to talk up the bakery and catering service, I'd be okay with that. Who knows? After this, I may have enough money just to work at the bakery."

"I can do word-of-mouth advertising. I'll put a standing order in for pastries because your temp job will be phased out." One hand went back to rub his neck, and then he nodded to someone behind Della.

Manners and curiosity turned her in the direction of the newcomer. "Oh, hi, Kyle."

"Hey, yourself," Kyle smirked and then gave Lawson a more

respectful nod. "Sir."

Jeffrey Lawson put down his plate to wrap one arm around Kyle's shoulder. "I'd like to introduce you to the new head of security. For his dedication to his job and diligence, I promoted him. Helps me out, too, because I needed leadership in the department since the previous head retired a few months ago."

"Congrats," Della told him and meant it. For the party, the man had donned a suit and wore it well. Maybe she'd been too quick to reject him for nattering on about a fantasy football league. After all, he was dependable, ambitious, and cleaned up well.

Someone called out to Lawson, making him drop his arm and turn to address the person. Della took a step closer. "He picked the right person for the job. Got any perks with the promotion?"

"Plenty. I get to work days. More money. It will look good on the resume, especially for the police academy." He pointed to himself with both thumbs. "Technically, I'll be the boss. Not the big boss, but the boss of my department."

He looked so pleased with the prospect that Della couldn't help but be delighted. She went up on tiptoes to give him a quick hug. "You deserve it."

"What's this?"

A shrill voice blasted Della's eardrum. She stumbled back, searching for the source. Close by, a slender woman in a tiny leopard patterned spandex dress, teetering on skyscraper heels and with equally tall hair, shot her a killing stare as she sauntered to Kyle's side. "Why is the help pawing my boyfriend?"

Boyfriend. The Help. Della wasn't sure which word grated more. She held her hands up as she retreated to the table. "Just congratulating him on the promotion."

"You're too late." The woman wagged a manicured finger in her face. "I got him. Run along and do your job."

As head of security, Kyle may have sensed an incident might be in the making. "Ah, honey, that's no way to be. Della is a co-worker. There's nothing between us."

Well, Della would have thought differently a few days ago when the man brought her tacos and roses. All the same, she did her best to reassure. "Absolutely, we just work together. You must be the girlfriend he's gushed about."

"I am Tifiani with three I's. How do you work with my sweet-heart and serve food, too?"

Della found herself explaining that she owned a bakery and catering service which sparked a speculative gleam in Tifiani's eyes. She dismissed her with a possible hint of calling her when they scheduled their big event. Since she didn't ask for a card, Della assumed she was blowing smoke. No biggie. She had a feeling Tifiani might give Ellie a run in the bridezilla department. Work called.

Della picked up a tray and cleared off the dirty dishes left on the serving table. The display still looked appetizing. An upbeat tune played as the deejay urged people to dance. Maybe things hadn't turned out the way she'd expected, but she noted the number of business cards missing from the display—a good sign. She didn't get the wedding of the decade, but this was a fine party that might yield future bookings and drop by customers. Things were looking up. Lawson slipped up beside her.

"Don't forget to check out that handsome Italian your mother has waiting for you," he teased.

"I'm almost afraid." She shook her head. Sometimes, she wondered why she even picked the name Cupid's Catering Company since she was so against falling in love. She supposed the name appealed to those in love or who hoped to be. Those folks didn't mind dropping major money to celebrate a birthday, anniversary, engagement, or a wedding.

Later that night after cleaning up and hauling the pots and pans to the bakery for a good soak, Della agreed to accompany her mother to Clarice's where Antonio was currently visiting, which probably meant he was a relative.

Being tired, sweaty, and sporting hat hair from her chef cap, Della didn't care since she wasn't out to charm anyone. She'd say hello, goodbye, and be on her way. It might be enough to appease her mother, but she wasn't ready for the sight that greeted her in Clarice's kitchen—an aristocratic nose, deep brown eyes, a ready smile, and four slender legs with delicate paws.

"I found him in the shelter," Mabel gestured to the dog. "I decided what I needed was a male of the canine variety when I saw this fellow. They said he was some Italian dog breed. Maybe greyhound, but he's not too big. I think he'll be a wonderful addition to the family."

On this, Della could agree.

The End.

FUDGY CHOCOLATE BROWNIE COOKIES

Prep Time: 10 minutes
Cook Time: 12 minutes
Total Time: 22 minutes
Servings: 16 cookies

Ingredients

- ½ cup unsweetened cocoa powder
- 1 cup white granulated sugar
- ½ cup melted butter
- 3 tablespoons vegetable oil
- 1 egg
- 2 teaspoons pure vanilla extract
- 1 1/3 cups all-purpose flour (or plain flour)
- ½ teaspoon baking powder
- ½ teaspoon salt
- 1/3 cup semi-sweet chocolate chips, (add more if desired) *

Instructions

1. Preheat oven to 350°F (175°C). Line 2 cookie sheets or baking trays with parchment paper (baking paper).
2. In a medium-sized bowl, mix the cocoa powder, white sugar, butter, and vegetable oil. Beat in egg and vanilla until fully incorporated.
3. Add the flour, baking powder, and salt. Stir the dry ingredients first before mixing them through the wet ingredients until a dough forms (do not overbeat). Fold in the chocolate chips.
4. Scoop out 1-2 tablespoonful of dough with a cookie scoop (or small ice cream scoop), and place onto prepared baking sheets. Press them down as thick or thin as you want your cookies to come out.
5. Bake in hot preheated oven for 10-12 minutes. The cookies will come out soft from the oven but will harden up as they cool. (Be careful not to over bake as they will dry out.)
6. Allow cooling on the cookie sheet for 10 minutes before transferring to wire racks for additional cooling.

* Spend more on quality chocolate chips for a better flavor.

Pumpkin Harvest Muffins

Prep Time: 20 minutes

Cook Time: 22 minutes

Total Time: 42 minutes

Servings: 12 Muffins

Ingredients

- 1 3/4 cup all-purpose flour
- 1 cup sugar
- ½ cup dark brown sugar
- 1 teaspoon baking soda
- ½ teaspoon salt
- 2 teaspoon cinnamon
- 1/4 teaspoon ground cloves
- 1/4 teaspoon nutmeg
- 2 eggs
- 1 15 ounce can pure pumpkin puree
- ½ cup coconut oil, melted
- 1 teaspoon vanilla extract.

Instructions

1. Preheat the oven to 375 degrees and place 12 paper liners into each well of your standard size muffin baking pan.
2. Measure out the flour, sugars, baking soda, salt, and spices in a medium bowl and whisk together. Set aside.
3. In another bowl, whisk together the eggs, pumpkin puree, coconut oil, and vanilla extract.
4. Pour the wet ingredients into the dry ingredients and stir together. Do not over mix, just stir until everything is incorporated into the batter.
5. It is helpful to use a large scoop (like an ice cream scoop) to evenly distribute the batter into each well. They will be nearly full. This will help give your muffins a nice puffy dome.
6. Bake your muffins for 20-22 minutes or until a toothpick inserted into the center of a muffin comes out clean.

Delish Orange Scones

Prep Time: 30 minutes
Cook Time: 15 minutes
Total Time: 45 minutes
Servings: 16 Medium Scones

Ingredients

For the Scones
- 1/4 cup granulated sugar
- zest from one large orange
- 3 cups all-purpose flour
- 3/4 teaspoon salt
- 1 tablespoon baking powder
- 4 ounces cream cheese, cold
- 6 tablespoons unsalted butter, cold
- 2 large eggs
- 1/3 cup milk
- 2 teaspoons vanilla extract
- 1 teaspoon orange extract

For the Orange Glaze
- 2 cups confectioners' sugar
- 4 tablespoons orange juice
- 1 teaspoon orange extract
- Orange zest of one large orange

Instructions

For the Scones:
1. Preheat oven to 425°. Line a baking sheet with parchment paper.
2. In a medium mixing bowl add sugar and orange zest. Rub together with your fingers until fragrant. Add to the flour, salt, and baking powder. Whisk together with sugar mixture. Place the cold cream cheese, butter, and eggs into the bowl of a food processor (I used a 14-cup processor), add dry ingredients. Pulse a couple of times or until combined. Pour in the milk, vanilla, and orange extracts. Pulse to mix. Remove dough from the processor onto a lightly floured surface. Divide the dough into 2 equal pieces. Form each piece into a 6-inch disk. Use a sharp knife to cut each disk into triangles. Place on a prepared baking sheet. Bake 15 minutes or until golden.
3. Lay a piece of wax paper under a wire cooling rack. Move baked scones to the wire cooling rack. Spoon or dip orange glaze over scones.

For the Orange Glaze:
1. In a medium bowl add the sugar, orange juice, orange extract, and orange zest. Whisk until smooth.

Buttermilk Pie

Prep Time: 10 minutes

Cook Time: 60 minutes**

Total Time: 70 minutes**

Servings: 8 slices

Ingredients

- 3 eggs
- ½ cup butter, softened
- 1 ½ cups white sugar
- 3 tablespoons all-purpose flour
- 1 cup buttermilk
- 1 teaspoon vanilla extract
- 1 tablespoon lemon juice
- ⅛ teaspoon freshly grated nutmeg
- 1 (9 inch) unbaked pie crust

Instructions

1. Preheat oven to 350 degrees (175 degrees C).
2. Beat eggs until frothy; add butter, sugar, and flour. Beat until smooth.
3. Stir in buttermilk, vanilla, lemon juice, and nutmeg; pour into pie shell.
4. Bake for 40 to 60 minutes, or until the center is firm

** Time varies with ovens.

Truffle Me Not

Chapter One

S MOOTH JAZZ PLAYED in the front of the bakery muffling the rattle of chairs being pulled out and jackets wiggled on. Della executed a playful dance step as she carried another tray of scones to the oven. A month ago, she wouldn't have bothered to keep baking past eight in the morning, aware that her gourmet goodies might still be on display at the end of the day. Laughter slipped in from the shop area. That's what she wanted to hear along with the ding of the cash register—only they didn't use an actual cash register, but more of a pad device that made no sound. Come to think of it, people hardly used cash, but instead relied on bank cards, credit cards, and often their phones to make purchases. No matter. As long as they kept coming with their plastic, all was right with Della's world.

A contented sigh escaped despite the sight of a sink crowded with dirty pans. Thanks to Jeffrey Lawson, the biggest employer in the area spreading the word about her bakery, she managed to climb out of the red. Even hired a part-time employee, Stephanie, who she met while trying to locate the missing heir. That was all behind them now. Life was good. Much better than she anticipated when she was in high school.

Even though it was more than a decade ago, every now and then, the memories of not quite fitting in no matter what she did came back. Her school broke down into cliques with the predominant ones being jocks, popular kids, and the hipsters, plus everyone else that didn't merit a label. As for the jocks, their name said it all while the popular kids were a little harder to define. Sure, it was easy to know who they were, but what made them popular was a little harder to define. Most came from powerful, affluent families that usually had a member on the school board. This often translated into good roles in the school play or being on the starting string in athletics.

Della's father as a detective had been well known, which made everyone give her the side-eye now and then, especially if they happened to be talking about underage parties. Every party that was busted somehow got laid on Della's doorstep. Never mind the fact her detective father didn't bother with underage drinking. It was assumed she told. Not sure how, since she was never invited. Not once did they ever consider loud music, the abundance of cars, and raucous behavior might have resulted in irate neighbors calling the police.

Some kids might have let it go, but not Lacey. Just her name had Della gritting her teeth. Small town life had its share of mean girls who grew up into entitled mean women, but Lacey had to be the queen of them all. For most, being beautiful, wealthy, and pretty much the topic of most conversations would be enough. Then there was her handsome fiancée she'd met somewhere in New England while vacationing. Even with everyone treating the woman like royalty, Della could tolerate it if her royal meanness stayed far, far away.

"Oh, how quaint!" A woman's condescending tone reached into

the kitchen and might as well have pinched Della. Her head jerked up and the pan she was scrubbing slipped from her fingers. A shiver raced up her spine. No, it couldn't be. Better check it out to be sure. There had to more than one snotty female in town. Her athletic shoes allowed her to creep across the kitchen floor without making a sound. Whoever was out there would say something else, dispelling the possibility it was Lacey. Why would Lacey even visit her modest bakery?

Stephanie explained the various delectable treats in an upbeat fashion that made her so good at her job. "Wouldn't you rather taste the food as opposed to taking pictures?"

Weird. Why would a person come in and take photos? Something wasn't right. Certain apps allowed people to snap a photo of an item and compare the prices of competitors. Well then, her photographer would soon discover Cupid's Catering Company had the best prices in town. Maybe she wanted a specialty item made?

If so, there were plenty of examples on the website. Della placed her palm on the door, ready to explain as much to the shopper. As the door swung open under her hand, it revealed Lacey Dankworth in a full-length fur coat that was inappropriate for the temperate November temps. The woman made a disdainful sniff as if the idea of sampling a cookie had to be a joke.

"Oh, no! I don't want to eat any of it." Her nose wrinkled and she took a step back, swaying slightly on her stiletto-heeled boots.

The woman made it sound like everything was poisoned. Della fisted her hands trying to remember as a merchant, a customer deserved her attention and best manners. So far, Lacey hadn't bought a thing, but she had gathered the attention of customers who were previously enjoying their pastries and coffee. A small petty part of Della wished the woman would lose her balance on her skyscraper heels. Off to Lacey's left stood an unassuming woman who leaned forward to grab her arm, possibly assuming a fall could be imminent.

"Rue!" Lacey addressed the helpful woman with scorn. "Let go of my arm. If you don't know how to act, go wait in the car."

The name sounded somewhat familiar. Della turned it over in her mind trying to place it with a younger face from their high school days. The woman in question dropped her grip and slunk to the front door, giving a last look over her shoulder before exiting. It didn't do her much good since Lacey paid no attention, being in full performance mode.

She addressed Stephanie but briefly glanced at Della as she spoke. "*I'm* going to open a bakery." Her glossy lips parted in a grin as she pressed her hands together. "Daddy said I could. I came here to see what I didn't want it to be." She gestured to the seated patrons. "You'll all want to come because it'll be the best. It will be sweet like me." Lacey said the words totally straight-faced. "Sweet Treasures. Remember the name. It'll be the *in* place to be."

With that, she pivoted sharply, swaying, before she caught her balance, then strutted to the door. Once there she waited, possibly expecting someone to open it for her. No one did.

The bell jingled as the door closed and Stephanie growled. "Don't know her. Don't like her and I wished she would have fallen off her ridiculous shoes."

While Della had a similar thought for a brief second, as a business owner, she couldn't afford any well-deserved accidents on her premises. "I'm grateful she didn't. It would end up being my fault, that much I do know."

What she didn't add was she knew Daddy Dankworth would pull out all the stops for his little princess to have a glitzy bakery if that's what her little heart desired. Since money was no object, she'd probably have some grand opening where she gave stuff away. People would be rushing to the place because that's how people acted around the beautiful people. Della closed her eyes remembering only moments before, life was good before Lacey chose Cupid's Catering Company to mock. "Why my bakery?"

"How do you know it's just yours?" Stephanie asked with an arched eyebrow. "I'm willing to bet she'd hit every place in town to spread her *sweetness*."

On that point, Della could agree. "I know money is no object for the Dankworths. They'll be able to afford equipment I can't touch for a while."

A few of the customers exited. A group of older women, who were friends of her mother's, gestured her over. No telling what they might want, but Della forced a smile as she headed in their direction trying to recall their names. Martha, Mary, and she couldn't quite get the third woman's name, but it was something she should know.

As she reached the table, the cotton-topped Mary reached for her hand and gave it a squeeze. "Don't worry about that spoiled brat. Her parents never did her any favors, giving her whatever she wanted. The girls..." she angled her head to the two remaining women, "couldn't help overhearing what Lacey said. Do you know why people go to bakeries?"

Baked goods felt like the right answer, but it might be a trick question. Della tried out a few more possibilities in her head, but Mary, tired of waiting, answered herself. "It's the quality of the goods. Sure, you can buy cheap cakes and cookies at the grocery.

The selection is limited and the quality mediocre. People who want something decent go to bakeries. Those who don't make it usually start out by charging too much or not providing consistent quality."

Having said her say, she dropped Della's hand and gave an emphatic nod. While both reasons for bakery failing were probable, she left out the major one—no one showing up because they are at another bakery. "I appreciate your interest and your patronage."

The woman whose name she couldn't remember held up her index finger. "You need to maintain attention on yourself. A baking contest of sorts."

That had merit, but only if she won. "I couldn't sponsor one and be in it at the same time."

"True," the woman agreed and glanced at her friends, who nodded. "That settles it. *We'll* sponsor it. Call it a charity. We can give any money earned to the local animal shelter. By the way, what do you consider your best item?"

Her fudgy chocolate cookies and orange scones were very popular, but she'd recently perfected her hot chocolate truffle with a creamy, rich chocolate body, and the tiniest bite of cayenne at the end. "I guess it would be my truffle."

"Okay." The woman shouldered her purse and stood. "Looks like we're having a truffle contest. I better get to work."

Mary and Martha waved at their departing friend. "Bye, Mimi. See you at the Friends of the Library meeting."

Oh yeah, *that* was her name. How likely was it that three women all with M names would be friends? If she counted her mother, Mabel, then it would be four women. Weird.

Della shrugged her shoulders dismissing the name mystery. Now, all she had to do was win the contest. With any luck, Lacey wouldn't hear about it. Enough money could buy an out-of-town pastry chef to compete for Sweet Treasures. Pastry chef or not, Della felt her truffles should win if it was a blind taste test. The assumption should have brought her comfort, but when it came to Lacey, nothing ever worked out in Della's favor.

Author Notes

Cupid Catering Company is my first catering cozy mystery series. I've spent a great deal of my life cooking with family and for work. The possibility of a mother and daughter running a catering business appealed. Like all families, there would be some issues on which they didn't hold the same views. While daughter, Della, may not always agree with her mother, Mabel, she is respectful of her parent. The two genuinely love and look out for each other. For a change, the characters aren't based on anyone in my family, but the cooking is.

The culinary aspects are courtesy of my grandmother plus my own experiences. My grandmother taught herself to cook and became quite well known for her pies. This talent kept her family fed since she spent her early morning hours at a bakery making bread, cookies, donuts, and pies for the day. I on the other hand worked in dietary at a local nursing home where I sometimes cooked for three hundred plus people. It became a running joke that I couldn't make anything for less than a hundred folks.

My husband, who is a software engineer, helped with the software or should I say middleware twist. Writing this book resulted in much baking, eating, and possibly five extra pounds.

I love to hear from and meet readers. Due to our recent health crisis, I will not be making any personal appearances at this time. In the meantime, stay in touch via my newsletter. Sign up at www.morgankwyatt.com.

Subscribers find out about exclusive freebies, contests, and personal appearances.

If you feel like writing a review, please do.

Reading takes you to your happy place. We need happy moments now more than ever.

MK Scott

www.morgankwyatt.com

Made in the USA
Las Vegas, NV
15 June 2023

73470643R00125